Ela Danforth seeks sanctuary in the small town of Rockypoint, New Hampshire, where she believes her days will return to normal, until a mysterious stalker threatens her refuge, just as a charming lawyer, Nash McCain, enters her life.

PRAISE FOR NORA LeDuc

MURDER CAME CALLING: "A Night Owl Romance Book Review TOP PICK!"

~*~

"*STAGING MURDER* absolutely kept me glued to my ereader. I was caught up in the suspense, quite curious about the murder, the threats and what they all meant for Ava."

~Jennifer Porter, Romance Novel News

~*~

"Impressively crafted, *PICK UP LINES FOR MURDER* is an enjoyable suspense thriller."

~Josee Morgan, Apex Reviews

~*~

MURDER BY HEART: "Tension begins on the first page and doesn't end until an unexpected culprit is revealed in the last few pages. This cleverly crafted story is filled with sexual tension that neither the hero nor the heroine wants to recognize and an abundance of action as they try to outwit a vicious killer."

~ Donna M. Brown for Romantic Times Book Reviews

~*~

LOVE'S WICKED JEWEL: "Several of the scenes contain wry humor that binds all into a tidy bundle of compelling and suspenseful romance."

~Faith V. Smith, Romantic Times Book Reviews

Trust Me

Nora LeDuc

TRUST ME

Copyright © 2014 by Nora LeDuc

Contact Information: NoraLeDuc@yahoo.com

Cover Art by cheryl@ccrbookcoverdesign.com
Digital Formatting by Author E.M.S.

Publishing History 2014
Digital ISBN: 978-0-9892090-4-5

Published in the United States of America

DEDICATION

To Lanie, may all your future dreams come true. Thanks for your
friendship, your stories and support. You are gold. Give Nash a
kiss for me. And to Kathleen, a million thanks for your insights.
I wish you a billion blessings.
~Love, Nora.

CHAPTER 1

"Daa-ad, we're almost at Dead Man's Curve." Nashua McCain's nine-year-old daughter Lanie leaned against the seatbelt and squinted through the passenger's windshield into the night. "You can barely see out the window," she warned him. "It's dangerous."

At the note of concern in her voice, Nash's fatherly instinct jumped into action. "Excellent point." He hit the button on the dashboard of his two-seater sports car. The defroster's hum grew louder and mixed with the wiper blades' rhythmic beat.

The cell phone in his leather jacket rang out the crescendo from his favorite movie score—a thriller.

"It's Grandma's ring," Lanie said. "You should stop and answer her. It's not safe to talk on your cell and drive at the same time. Grandma tells Grandpa that all the time when he drives."

"Who's raising you, the Grandmothers' Safety Council?" His daughter was nine going on fifty. Why did that worry him? Maturity was good, wasn't it? But she was right. Too many deaths had occurred on this bend in the road, and ever since his wife had died, Lanie had assumed the role of the cautious family member, fearing real or imaginary harms.

He braked and steered toward the parking area on the side that was designed for tourists to take photos of the distant White Mountains or the village of Rockypoint, New Hampshire lying below. Tonight, the early spring rainstorm blotted out the lights from the valley's thirteen thousand residents.

He shifted into park, flicked his flashers and flipped the

1

button of the overhead light before he clicked the cell's button. "Hello, Mother."

"Happy birthday, Nashua. You aren't driving in this torrential downpour with Lanie, are you?"

"Good to hear from you, Mom. Thanks for the birthday greeting." He shrugged at Lanie as the rain won the battle of the fogged front glass. Headlights from behind popped out of the night and bounced off his rearview mirror. He averted his gaze.

"Your routine is as predictable as your father's fussing when he opens our tax bill," his mother continued. "This is the day and hour when you visit that little bar you call a café for supper. It's not the place for a little girl, not that you care for my opinion."

"Yes, we're on our way to eat at my favorite café like we do every year on the first of April. And it's a coffee bar owned by our friends from church."

"Why don't you come for dinner Sunday? We can celebrate together, and I've a special friend you should meet."

Danger. She always *invited* him when she'd found a "friend" to introduce. She couldn't understand that he preferred to find his own dates and keep relationships casual. He made an effort to filter the frustration out of his tone as he answered, "I'll check my schedule and let you know."

"Your father told me you're free."

Lanie tugged on his sleeve. "Dad. Dad. Look at those cars!" She pointed behind her. Her fingers tightened with urgency on his arm. Four advancing headlights side by side sped up the hill. "They're headed for Dead Man's Curve. They're going too fast and going to crash."

"I've gotta go, Mother." Nash dropped the phone in the cup holder.

The two vehicles flew towards them, neck and neck on the two-way road. Micro inches separated them. They shot past Nash. Their red rear lights burned through the dark, slashing rain. He narrowed his eyes and distinguished the shape of a pickup's bed on one vehicle, now attempting to pass the other. Sure enough, it smacked against the driver's side of what looked like an early sixties car. The screech of metal against metal broke through the rain pounding on his sports car's roof. The vintage car swerved onto the shoulder, and for a split second, it balanced on the edge of the winding pavement before it plummeted over the side of the nine-hundred-foot drop.

With a shot of backfire, the white truck roared off.

"Dad! Can you believe that? He drove someone off the road and left! What's going to happen? Are they dead?" Lanie's hoarse whisper broke the silence. She unsnapped her seatbelt and bent forward to wipe the fog off the window with the cuff of her aqua fleece jacket and stared after the pinpoint of crimson taillight disappearing around the peak's curve.

"We'll report it. Get the driver help. Everyone will be okay." He hoped.

"It was a hit and run. Right?" She blinked her hazel eyes. The freckles on her nose and cheeks stood out on her ashen face.

"Yes, it was." Did he look as scared as she did? It didn't feel real. He wanted to replay the scene in his mind with a different ending.

"Do you think anybody is alive? What if they had kids?" She tucked her brown hair into her collar and scooted toward the door.

"I'll call for help."

He grabbed the phone and within seconds reported the accident to nine-one-one. The operator continued with questions, but he had to go down to that car.

"Just a minute," he told the woman and handed the cell to his daughter. "I need you to do this important thing for me. Stay here and talk to the emergency operator while you watch for the ambulance and police. I'll find out what happened to the driver. Got it?"

"What if you fall?"

"I'm only going down a little way to see if anyone's hurt and will come right back." He opened the glove compartment and snatched his flashlight. "Set?"

"Don't be gone long." She raised the phone to her ear. "Hello."

From the console, he removed his Red Sox cap and stuffed it on his head. Outside, the raindrops pelted his face and struck the pavement around him. He yanked up the collar of his jacket. Ahead, the twisted and broken guardrail marked where the vehicle had gone off. He sprinted to the spot and climbed over the remains of the metal railing. He steadied on the rim of the precipice and looked down through the sheet of rain into the darkness. With his beam he scanned the hill dotted with protruding granite, scraggly, barren trees and brush. Could anyone survive such a crash? At least he didn't spot flames. Nash murmured a prayer that someone would live.

He began to inch down the forty-five degree slope. He paused to allow the soles of his running shoes to grip the slick, uneven ground of rock and edged past the trees. Their jutting roots acted as speed bumps on the wet ground.

Who would race up Moose Hill in a dead heat and force another person off the hillside? A drunk driver? An angry spouse?

Nash's sneakers slid on the slippery, hard surface, and he slowed his descent. What else could he expect from living in a place nicknamed the Granite State? Sweat beaded his forehead. What was he thinking? Coming down here was risky. The starless darkness and sheets of water closed around him and cut off his visibility. He had to rely on the limited glow from his flashlight. Already, his jeans were soaked. The shower penetrated his clothing and trickled down the inside of his neckline, coolness touching his skin, and he was only one-third of the way down.

A soft moan drifted up to him. Was he imagining the noise? The sound floated uphill again. Someone was alive below him, at least for the moment.

He ran his beam across the ground and caught sight of a body of an upside-down vehicle. Its trunk and engine were wedged between two trees. He picked up his speed and skidded down the last few yards to the car. "Hello? Can you hear me?" He froze to listen through the torrent.

A groan answered him.

"Dad! Dad!"

Lanie? She stood at the edge of the hillside. All he needed was his daughter falling down the hill. He cupped his hands to his mouth. "Stay up there."

"Did you find anyone? Are you coming back?"

"Don't move." Fear raised his voice.

"Hel—p." The single word wafted from the auto.

He ran to the crumpled metal side, crouched down and flashed his light on a young woman with blonde hair hanging in the overturned vehicle. The safety harness and airbag imprisoned her in the driver's seat. She stared straight ahead, unaware of him. At least he didn't spot blood, and no one else was inside. "The ambulance is on the way. Hold on. Are you hurt?"

Her eyelids flickered shut.

A siren wailed in the distance.

"Hello? The emergency workers are almost here. You'll be okay."

Maybe they weren't soon enough. He yanked on the door handle. Nothing budged.

* * *

"Are you Nash McCain?"

From his place beside the hallway snack machines, Nash lowered the paper cup of tepid coffee from his lips. It was the third he'd had in the nearly two hours since he arrived at the hospital. He should have insisted Lanie go to her grandmother's house, but they'd both been delayed by the police for interviews and their hospital visit to check on Suz Danforth's condition.

A lean, cinnamon-haired woman with a mass of curls stood in front of him. The fluorescent light revealed lines of fatigue in an otherwise striking face. He had to remind himself not to stare.

She was about a foot taller than Lanie's four feet, with high cheekbones and an ivory complexion that suggested a delicate nature, but the upward thrust of her jaw and firm eye contact denoted strength.

"I'm Michaela, or Ela Danforth. You helped my sister tonight." She extended a hand.

He moved closer to her. For a second, she tensed her shoulders and then she relaxed and shook his hand. "It's nice to meet you, Miss Danforth." She was about twenty-six or seven. In her black pants and top, she seemed ready for grieving. The dark circles under her large brown eyes made him want to offer aid and assure her tomorrow would be better. "We should move to the waiting room and grab a chair."

"I'll only take a minute." She swallowed and straightened her back. "The nurse mentioned you were in the hall. I'd like to thank you for helping Suz. The police informed me she was fortunate you found her and directed the rescue personnel. She could have been trapped down there for hours without anyone noticing."

"I'm glad I could do something, but the emergency workers are the heroes."

Your sister couldn't get out of her car." Lanie popped up from beside the candy machine. "They used the jaws of life to pry her loose."

He laid a hand on her shoulder and raised his brows to signal her to stop talking. "Lanie."

Ela moistened her full lips. "You were in the right place when she needed you. I don't know how to express my gratitude."

"My dad climbed down the hillside to save her," Lanie said, focused on Ela and oblivious to him. "I'm Elaine, but everyone calls me Lanie. Want one?" She waved a red licorice twist, and the scent of strawberry blended with the hallway's sterile antiseptic odor.

"Thanks." The woman hesitated and then took the candy and held it in her fist as if it were a lifeline. "I'm pleased to meet you." The crinkle in her forehead disappeared.

"I talked to nine-one-one, too," Lanie said. Her face glowed with pride.

"That's enough," Nash reminded her with a gentle squeeze of her shoulder.

Lanie lowered her head and peeked upward at her father, as if trying to judge how much trouble she was in.

"I appreciate both your help." Ela offered her hand to Lanie.

The young girl beamed with happiness.

"How's your sister doing?" he asked.

"Suz is with the doctor who set her broken leg. Since she suffered a lot of bruises and lost consciousness, she will stay overnight for observation."

"Her guardian angel was watching over her," Lanie said. "I'll keep praying for her."

The lines returned to the woman's face, and she retreated a step. She seemed to run hot and cold, but then if someone Nash loved was hospitalized, his reactions might be unpredictable, as well.

"If you'll excuse me, I'll return to my sister's room to wait for the nurse to bring her in."

"Did the police offer an idea or theory about the truck?" he asked, to keep her from leaving. His heart thudded an extra beat in anticipation of spending more time with her, even if it wasn't his best idea. Then he would get to know her and probably like her—maybe even a lot—and he'd vowed, after what happened with his wife, Cindy, that he'd never get that close to a woman again.

"They should hurry up and catch that truck driver," Lanie interjected, "before he runs away. Dad thinks so too."

Ela's mouth fell open. "You don't believe it was an accident and that the driver panicked and sped away?"

"Didn't the police speak to you?" Nash asked.

She bit her lip and shrugged. "An officer told me they're exploring the possibility my sister became involved in a drag racing accident. I don't know much else."

"The driver in the truck knocked your sister off the curve on purpose," Lanie announced.

The woman flinched at the last words.

"Lanie, we're not CSI. The police will handle the investigation. I'm sorry, Miss Danforth. It's a stressful night for you." What more could he do to help her? Aha—Nash pulled his card from his pocket and offered it to her.

As she took it, their hands brushed and there it was—that zing of attraction. Her eyes widened with awareness.

He cleared his throat before speaking. "I'm a trial attorney. I'm also an insomniac who loves to tempt people to stay on the phone with me during the late, boring hours by offering free advice. Take advantage and call me. In a small town, I've many kinds of cases and I've become savvy on numerous categories of the law." He grinned, hoping to ease her pained expression.

"You're a lawyer?" She held his card away from her as though he'd presented her with a bottle of arsenic. "I have to leave now."

She turned and walked away. The sound of her heeled footsteps echoed in the snack area.

Lanie leaned toward him. "She didn't like your business card, Dad, and didn't pay any attention when I talked about a guardian angel."

"I'm afraid not everyone thinks my profession is useful. Though anyone with common sense wants an angel on her shoulder." He wrapped his arm around her. "Let's go call Grandma and ask her if we can stop by for dessert. The bag of peanuts didn't fill me up."

"We never ate supper."

"I won't tell if you don't."

Lanie smiled and skipped ahead to the red exit sign. Outdoors, the storm had subsided. They walked to their car near the emergency entrance. Lanie babbled on about the adventures of the evening. Nash's thoughts were on Ela Danforth and her strange reactions to his offer of support and Lanie's mention of a guardian angel.

Ela had his interest, for sure, but her warm then cool behavior reminded him too much of his deceased wife. His policy now was to stay away from deep emotional entanglements with women.

Today might be April Fool's Day, but at age thirty-six, he'd smartened up.

* * *

Ela stepped into the cool night air and hovered by the hospital's well-lit entrance. The rain had quit, but dampness thickened the air. When she and her sister inherited Aunt Vickie's house and store, she'd thought their lives would be on an upswing. But her mother jetted off to Europe, and Suz had come to live with Ela. The decade between them seemed more like a century when Ela tried to reason with her teenaged sister about school, home and Tyler Rawlings. One moment Suz was in love with him, and the next, she hated him. Dealing with the emotional highs and lows of a teen left Ela drained.

And no matter how far she went, she couldn't shake her past. She'd felt uneasy when the police chief acknowledged he was familiar with her father's arrest in New York, thanks to the national media. She should have guessed a man of the law would be aware of the trials that hit the national news circuit.

She wished she could turn back time to the days before the nightmare with her father, when Aaron Wright and she were first engaged, and his family members were around to support and protect her.

The cry of a baby drifted out of the building and pulled her back to reality. No use dreaming about Aaron and her almost extended family.

Anyway her sister was alive, and she owed her future to a lawyer. Nash was handsome, tall and athletic-looking—a heartbreaker. But she'd met plenty of his type in Manhattan during her father's ordeal and her knowledge of his kind lessened her attraction. These guys used their good looks and promises of big wins to lure women and men into hiring them. Nash had offered to be a sounding board for free, but he must expect payment in some form, eventually. She'd skip his offer.

Besides, a man in her life right now was a terrible idea. Her father, his lawyers and Aaron had all let her down in a big way. At least she'd protected Aaron's dad, who would have been devastated if she'd revealed his son's plan—or so she told herself when guilt nipped at her for keeping his last secret.

As for Nash, she'd experienced gratitude mixed with a touch of infatuation since he'd saved Suz's life. He'd been the hero of the evening. His hazel eyes surfaced in her mind and refused to leave. They had been different. They were full of curiosity, compassion and—

Her phone rang. Splitting her concentration between her musings and the incoming call, she dug out the cell from her pocket.

"The Lord will punish the world for their evil, and the wicked for their iniquity. You must repent and forgive or you will suffer—"

She hit the off button. Her body shook. If her mind hadn't been in overdrive, she'd never have answered without checking the caller ID. What should she do now? What would *he* do next?

CHAPTER 2

"You idiot," Money Bags shouted over the phone. "You messed up everything, and now the police are asking questions. I'm not paying you one cent after what you did."

"Huh?" He jerked the cell an inch from his ear and navigated the bumpy back road with one hand on the wheel. "The paper printed a story about the Moose Hill accident on the front page. Didn't you see it? Are you trying to cheat me?"

"Read the caption under the picture of the smashed Chevy. That's the little letters that form words."

He stole a glance at the newspaper lying on the passenger seat of his truck. "What!" He steered to the breakdown lane, grabbed the first section and read.

"The survivor of the Dead Man's Curve accident has been identified as sixteen-year-old Suzanne Danforth." He paused and reread the words and then cleared his throat. "We've a little setback."

"Did your parents give you a brain? It's a major fiasco. Smarten up."

He imagined the spit shooting out of Money's mouth. He tossed the paper on the floor mat. "I'll fix everything. Save your cash. I'll be collecting."

"You'd better fix your mistake if you want to be paid, and no more car accidents. The police are looking for your truck. Get rid of it and don't forget to dump your prepaid phone, too. I'll send you a new one."

"I'm on it."

"And no witnesses, whatever you do. I'll be watching for

results. If you don't come through, I guarantee you a lot of pain."

The click in his ear told him Money Bags had hung up.

Money didn't own him. He'd take care of everything when he wanted and have a little fun doing it. Right now, he had to stop at the pet store. He needed lunch for his snake.

* * *

Once she left the hospital, Ela spent part of the night trying to escape her problems by staying busy in the kitchen. She finally fell asleep close to morning. Now she awoke in the lilac wallpapered bedroom once reserved for Aunt Vickie's guests. Gray light poured through the tall windows. She tossed onto her back in the black-iron-framed bed and yanked up the cream coverlet. A rose sachet scent tugged at her senses.

The memory of her last dream drained from her consciousness. She grasped hold of it. Men in business suits surrounded her chair at the long table. They spoke in hushed voices while jotting notes and assessed her with cold, dark eyes. Then they blurred together in kaleidoscope fashion, replaced by Nash McCain's concerned hazel eyes staring down at her. She blinked and forced the images away.

A sense of loss and loneliness shrouded her. She lay still, drowning in the feelings. No, she couldn't—wouldn't go there. She flinched at the ring of the phone. What if *he* was calling? Ela's heart thudded louder with each ring. If Suz found out the calls had started again, she'd flip. Ela wouldn't answer and give *him* the joy of preaching to her.

But it could be the hospital. She threw back the coverlet. The weave of the multi-colored Oriental rug warmed the soles of her feet. Suz was right. They needed to get into the twenty-first century with caller ID on the landline. Ela seized the receiver of the rotary style phone sitting on the marble-topped nightstand.

"Hello, baby, are you ready to make up and be friends?"

The rough whisper slid down her spine like a porcupine quill. "Who is this?"

"Suz, is that you?"

"Tyler?" She wrestled with the urge to hang up on her sister's boyfriend. They'd met the first day Suz attended high school in

Rockypoint, two months ago. Last night, while they'd been talking about Suz's accident and acquaintances, Police Chief Ballad warned her Tyler had been a suspect in a town theft. So far, no charges had stuck. Had he graduated to attempted manslaughter by running her sister off the road during one of their arguments?

"Who's this?" Tyler asked, interrupting her train of thought.

"This is Ela. Suz was in an accident last night."

"What do you mean?"

"She's in the hospital after surgery for a broken leg, a possible concussion and multiple bruises."

He let out a low whistle. "What happened?"

"She went off Dead Man's Curve on Moose Hill. The police are investigating."

"Was it around seven?"

"How did you know?" Ela sank onto on the edge of the mattress. Her hand dampened around the receiver.

"Suz called me about that time to let me know she was on her way. She never showed up."

"Why didn't you contact me when Suz was a no-show?" Ela stiffened.

"We had a fight when she called. She'd told me she couldn't come and then changed her mind and expected me to drop everything when it fit her schedule. She got mad and hung up."

"You must have been angry, too." Angry enough to jump in his truck and run her off the road? And he'd never checked on her. Great boyfriend.

"I can't believe she was in a wreck."

"A couple of witnesses reported a pickup was too close and knocked her off the curve."

Tyler snorted. "Did the cops give them a lie detector test? Lots of crazies out there make up stories to get attention."

"The police will verify their statements." Her to-do list didn't include feeding information to Tyler.

"Does Suz have a good doctor? When my dad's sick, he uses a neighbor who went to medical school in another country. No degree, but he's cheap. I'll talk to him."

Super idea. Suz needed a fake physician as much as she needed Tyler as a boyfriend.

"Did she tell you—"

"Your plan to live together after graduation? She did, and I don't support the idea. She'll be in her last year of high school next year. Tyler, seventeen is too young to move in together. You barely know each other." Ela had a hard time liking anyone who tried to talk her sister into making such a huge mistake.

"We're different from other people. We don't keep secrets from each other."

If only the problems in life were solved by sharing. "Wait a couple of years." *Or forever, until I'm certain you won't hurt Suz.* "Don't bother telling me about all the teens who live together. I'm not their big sister."

"When can we discuss this?" he asked with an eagerness she was definitely not feeling.

"When my sister turns eighteen, we'll talk."

"I know your problem. It's the money. Suz explained it to me. I told you—no secrets."

"People need cash to live, including you and my sister. Forget the idea. Right now, the police will want to interview you about the accident. I've got to go." Ela ended the call before he offered more opinions.

After their conversation, she wanted to turn on all the lights and hide her valuables. Instead, she'd jumped into the shower, and then dressed in gray pants and her favorite blue shirt. She snatched her umbrella from the closet.

Her thoughts turned to Nash McCain. She didn't need him as a lawyer, but she needed whatever he might have seen last night to find out if Suz was in trouble. Digging out his card, she headed for his downtown office three blocks from her neighborhood, where Victorian homes with their sprawling porches and bay windows could almost trick you into thinking life could be idyllic.

* * *

Nash sat at his desk in his five-by-seven foot office. His furniture crammed the closet-size room. The window overlooked a burger and fries restaurant across the street. Whiffs of fast food seeped inside when the wind blew toward their building. Nash's office was temporary while the landlord finished a facelift on the law firm's permanent home on the second floor, one flight beneath him. Despite the soundproofing, the whine of electric tools drifted through the wooden planks.

Lanie's smiling picture greeted him from across the desk. The sight of her face always flooded him with happiness, followed by a sharp pang of doubt. Her teachers reported she was smart and well behaved but had no close friends. His mother reminded him Lanie should be invited to get-togethers with children her age, but the invitations never came. Everyone assured him she could mix with her peers, but she preferred to spend recess speaking to the teachers and her free time with her family. She often sounded more like an adult than a child.

Despite his best efforts to encourage playmate interactions and ease her worries, she resisted. The guidance counselor advised baby steps at his daughter's pace. Too bad Lanie's speed appeared to be crawling.

Maybe he should be happy with her status. Lanie didn't appear to be on track to grow into a teenager who raced up Moose Hill like Suzanne Danforth. Her big sister Ela had her hands full.

Nash focused on Ela Danforth. He'd spent the night replaying their conversation in his mind. He recalled the way her curls flowed together into a full mane of hair and how her forehead crinkled when she frowned or worried. Yesterday, he'd resisted the urge to look for her online, but today, he gave into his curiosity. Shoving his swivel chair closer to his desk, he typed "Ela Danforth" into the screen's search box. He raised his hand to hit enter when the buzz of his intercom alerted him that his secretary, Joanne, on the other side of the closed door, wished to speak to him. He grabbed the receiver.

"Mr. Harrington, your first appointment, canceled. He called to say he's at the hospital having tests, and he's sure the results will help his case."

Harrington owned half the real estate in Rockypoint. Nash's father claimed winning him as a client was a coup for their law firm. Nash had set aside the two hours the man insisted he needed to discuss their strategies for his personal injury lawsuit, resulting from a car accident with a soon-to-be ex-friend. At their initial consultation, Harrington had proven himself to be an obnoxious know-it-all, but Nash didn't take cases based on personalities, as tempting as the idea was.

"Thanks, Joanne."

"I also have a Miss Ela Danforth here who would like to see you. She doesn't have an appointment."

He glanced at the search box on the monitor. "That was fast."

"Excuse me?"

"Send her in." He closed the program and rolled down his sleeves. The thought of seeing Ela again raised his spirits.

The door opened and the woman who'd haunted his night walked back into his life.

Color highlighted her cheeks, though shadows of weariness still framed those huge eyes. The fragrance of flowers surrounded her and reminded him of carefree summer days. His gaze skimmed down her raincoat to gray, hugging pants and high-heeled boots. She threw the hood off and revealed her mass of curly cinnamon hair.

His fingers flexed with the urge to touch it. He resisted the impulse and confirmed one fact about Ela Danforth: she was not the typical Rockypoint woman who wore jeans and added plastic fingernails for a special occasion. He pictured her attending affairs for rich museum patrons with servers and harp players.

He rose. "Good morning."

Her gaze swept over him and the room. She seemed to be sizing him up. "Sorry to drop in without an appointment. You must have a long list of them." She nodded at the piles of files on his desk.

"My first client canceled. Can I offer you a cup of coffee?" He edged around the narrow space near his desk to the coffeemaker sitting on a file cabinet.

"No, thanks. I have a tight agenda. I've already been to the police station and spoken with Police Chief Ballard, and from here, I'm on my way to the hospital."

"Ballard?" His old nemesis. He should have guessed he'd lead the case, since vehicular manslaughter went to the highest ranking officer on the force.

"Is there something I should know about him? You looked irritated." She bit her lip and waited for him to answer.

Making her anxious about the investigation was unfair.

Ballard did his job and held a clean record. Nash put on his inexpressive, lawyer face. "The chief and I have known each other since we played together on the high school basketball and baseball teams. He's aggressive, and he'll work your case day or night."

"That's good to hear. He's already cleared my friends and members of my book club. I don't think any of them drive over thirty on the back roads, which seems to eliminate them."

"They were suspects?"

"I've missed a meeting or two, but since I wasn't bringing the snacks, I'm sure they've no motives to hurt Suz." The corners of her mouth turned upwards.

A woman who possessed a sense of humor about her life. Each second, he liked her more. "Thanks for the tip. Have a seat." He motioned to the wooden chair near his desk. His mother had given him the furniture when he'd moved into his office. She insisted it was an antique worth lots of money. He suspected she'd bought it for almost nothing at one of her flea market haunts.

Ela sat and rested her hands on top of the purse balanced on her knees. "I brought a little something for you." She dug inside the oversized, black bag slung over her shoulder and produced a small, wrapped, golden box with a red bow. "It's not much compared to saving my sister's life."

"You didn't need to bring me anything. You thanked me last night." He sat behind his desk and set the gold box in front of him. "How's your sister doing?"

"Suz is talking, which is good and bad." She smiled faintly.

"Any news on who ran her off the road?"

Ela toyed with the band of her watch. "Suz doesn't remember much. Chief Ballard told me a couple of theories he's working on." She fell silent and seemed lost in her thoughts, staring over his head out the only window. From the street came the honk of car horns and from below the whine of a saw.

"Are you allowed to share them?" he asked. "Last night you mentioned something about a race at the hill."

She paused, as though she was censoring her words before she answered.

"I don't believe the chief's ideas are a secret. He thinks a race on the hill is possible. Another theory is that the accident was the result of road rage. Maybe Suz cut someone off. She's not the most observant driver since she's only had her license a month. Chief Ballard also suggested that since Suz and her boyfriend Tyler fought, he was trying to get even by scaring her last night. He might have meant to make her pull to the side and not over the hill. I remember he used his father's white truck once."

"Everyone in Rockypoint drives a truck."

"I've a lot to learn about your town. Anyway, the last premise seems unlikely. Tyler's never shown a violent or out of control side, and Suz told me an hour ago on the phone that Tyler sped to her bedside this morning and pledged his undying love. She also asserted that he'd rather be bit by a pack of rabid werewolves than hurt her." Ela tightened her lips as though she'd munched on a sour fruit.

"Why do I guess you're not a fan of your sister's boyfriend?"

"I'm not sure he's telling her the truth, but Suz believes him. She's only sixteen and he's seventeen. They're both in high school and think they'll be together forever. I may be misreading him, but I don't believe he's mature enough to handle a lifetime commitment. My sister isn't, and with all the upheaval in her life, Suz would like anyone who was nice to her."

"Do you have a jealous ex hiding somewhere, or a frenemy who wanted to get in a little payback?"

"I've no idea about Tyler's past relationships. My sister lives pretty much in the moment. When we moved to Rockypoint two months ago, she suffered from the usual transition problems, but cracking the high school code is tough for anyone. She's never mentioned a person in particular who gave her trouble."

He tapped his fingers on the desktop, absorbing the facts. "The police will investigate their friends. That's a given."

She pinned him with a direct stare. "I wondered if you could describe the truck driver involved in the accident."

"Sorry. Tinted windows, heavy rain and night conditions work against identifying suspects."

"What about height? What was your impression? Did the driver seem tall or short? Maybe your daughter noticed something."

"Neither Lanie nor I could ID a suspect. If we tried, a good lawyer would destroy us, given the weather and time of evening. What makes you think it was a man?"

"I guessed. I should go," she said, rising.

"One minute." He jumped up, sending his chair flying against the wall with a thud.

Her brows shot together as she paused in front of him.

He searched for a reason to delay her. His glance fell on the wrapped box. "I haven't opened your gift."

Her face flushed a rosy pink. "You don't need to unwrap it while I'm here. Besides, the present is kind of silly."

"Humor me and stay a second." He tore off the paper and opened the lid. Four irregularly shaped—obviously homemade pieces of chocolate nestled together on a white sheet.

"I told you it was nothing." She wound the purse strap around her palm.

The sugary scent rose and teased him to eat a piece. His mouth watered. "Did you make this fudge?"

"Yes, I often cook when I can't sleep. I hope you eat sweets."

"I love them—too much. I'm a bad example for Lanie. Thanks."

She dipped her head. "I wanted to show my appreciation for all you've done."

Something about the way she broke eye contact roused his curiosity. From the box, the candy called to him. Would a bite hurt? He bit into a square and closed his eyes. The soft, creamy substance melted on his tongue. "Miss Danforth, you're an angel."

"I know without a doubt that's untrue." She turned to leave. "Enjoy," she said over her shoulder.

"I'll escort you out." He rounded the desk while his common sense cautioned him to let her go. She'd come mainly for whatever information he could provide about the pickup truck and its driver.

"Oh, please, don't bother." She hesitated and waved a hand.

"Seeing you out isn't a problem."

She shrugged, as though she were out of excuses. He grabbed his jacket from a hook in the corner. In the carpeted waiting room, he spoke to Joanne at her desk and continued with Ela into the hallway scented with citrus air freshener. When they stopped in front of the elevator, he faced her. "You've lived in Rockypoint for two months, but we've never met."

"Do you know everyone in the town, Mr. McCain?" She narrowed her dark eyes at him.

"You must get around."

"In this town, everyone gets around to meeting each other sooner or later. You'll find out." That was lame, but true. He racked his mind for a recovery line. Why was he having trouble? He was good with words. He made his living by using them.

"We moved to Rockypoint when my aunt passed on and willed us her house. She ran an antique business downtown, Now and Then. Did you ever go to her shop?"

"I never did, but my mother loved the place. Did you reopen the store?"

"The shop's closed. I plan to sell the building. For now, I'm working at the library. I'm the person who wheels around the little cart. The job's temporary. I hope to get something else soon, especially since the high school kids, who they usually hire, refer to me as granny."

"No one would mistake you for a grandma." Was she kidding? The woman was in her late twenties at the most. "I spend a lot of time in the reference room. I'll probably run into you. The library's on the street right behind us. What was your profession?"

"I worked in the family business." She stepped away from him, and ended the conversation.

He tried to understand her reaction. Had he offended her or was she preoccupied? The ding announced the elevator's arrival. She strode across the threshold and blinked in surprise when he joined her inside the elevator car.

When they reached the first floor lobby, she paused by the entrance. "Thanks, Mr. McCain."

"The trip down was tough, but I aim to please." He opened the glass door and scanned the street. Pedestrians in light jackets hurried past on the sidewalks in front of the three- and four-story brick shop fronts. In the opposite direction, he spotted two uniformed firefighters washing one of the ladder trucks outside their garage. The men waved as vehicles passed by and beeped in greeting. "Where's your car?"

"You've forgotten. My car went off Dead Man's Curve and was totaled. Suz and I won't be driving for a while."

"Sorry, didn't you say you were visiting your sister next? The hospital is ten blocks away on the outskirts, and the meteorologist promised rain again. How'd you get to my office? Do you live nearby?"

"I got here the old-fashioned way. You may have heard of it. You move one foot in front of the other."

"I hear it's an ancient trend unpopular with our youth unless they're at the gym." He inclined his head toward the low-hanging gray clouds. "I'll drive you."

"But—"

"My bank is near the hospital, and I need to make a withdrawal. It'll be a two for one."

"You weren't on your way out a few minutes ago." The sound of her phone from inside her purse saved Nash from a quick reply.

Ela dug it out, glanced at the caller ID and shut it off. She clamped her hand around the cell as she shoved it into her pocket. Waves of invisible tension vibrated off her hunched shoulders.

"Are you okay?"

"I will be when I see Suz. Mr. McCain, I'll take that ride."

Whose ID had she read off her phone? "I'm parked in the rear, and my name's Nash. If you stay out front, I'll—"

"I'll walk with you, Nash." She smiled at him as though he'd offered her a winning lottery ticket. "Ready?"

That was a fast switch, he thought as they strolled off together. What was going on with Ela Danforth? Her moods swung from cold to sweet and unfriendly to friendly within a wink. Her behavior threw him back into the past and his problems with Cindy. He recalled middle of the day emergencies and the final call from the police asking him to come home at once. He'd prayed and fought hard for his wife. The doctors had, too. They'd predicted her moods would settle with the new meds. It was not to be.

As he and Ela reached his sports car, he pushed away the long-ago memories. Ela sat in the passenger seat and held the black purse on her lap like a shield. He tossed her umbrella behind the seats to give her room to stretch out.

"What does your wife think of your heroics last night?" she asked, staring straight ahead.

At least she was talking, though he would've chosen a different topic. "My wife passed away two and a half years ago."

She jerked her attention from the windshield. Her brown eyes reflected shock. "I'm sorry."

"If she were here, she'd agree I did what anyone in my circumstance would have done." The familiar ache in his chest had dulled enough that he could speak about his wife without intense pain. Most people called it progress. Nash called it loss.

He traveled away from the commercial part of town, its display windows plastered with signs promising pre-summer sales, toward the residential section of multi-colored one story houses. Forsythias graced most of the yards. Their new buds promised the long winter had passed. At the other end of road, he passed a series of pizza shops and cheap gas stations before taking a left at the large black-lettered sign that announced the Rockypoint Hospital.

"The press is here." She pointed toward the brick building.

He braked. Near the hospital's main entrance sat a van with the Channel 23 logo. A small group of men and women in fleece jackets and windbreakers lingered outside the doors. One young woman pushed a tot in a stroller back and forth near the front of the gathering. Various signs popped up in the crowd. A man carried a warning placard: *Rockypoint roads kill!*

Ela wrinkled her nose. "Why is a car crash big news?"

"The newspaper ran an article a month ago about the danger of Dead Man's Curve, along with an accident report that showed three deaths within the past five years occurred on that section of the bend. All the deceased were teenagers. Parents of the last victim formed an organization, Save Our Children, or SOC, to pressure the town to straighten the curve."

"No results yet?"

"Just the engineer's study indicating improvements would cost big bucks that Rockypoint can't afford. The town also maintains the road can't be changed. SOC argues blasting and rebuilding the two lanes' grade will increase safety on the incline and curve. I bet the organization wants to add your name and your sister's to its supporters' list. I'll drive you around to the side." He cruised past the protestors and stopped underneath the concrete canopy with the *Emergency* sign over it.

"Thanks. Next time, I'll whip up a bigger batch of fudge." She slung her purse over her shoulder.

"I appreciate it, but you don't owe me, Miss Danforth. I wish I could give you more information about your sister's accident." He leveled his gaze on her. She met his stare, and his pulse kicked up. He caught the hot spark of recognition in her eyes. Who was this woman who made fudge and was a fierce protector of her younger sister?

She ducked her head, breaking eye contact. "I know, and after last night, please call me Ela." She slid out of the car.

He should say something about seeing her again. "El—" her door banged shut, and she strode toward the entryway. "—la."

Maybe it was better he didn't get to know Ela Danforth. He was still too raw inside. He hit the accelerator and glanced in the rearview mirror. A man stepped out of the parking lot and jogged straight toward her. A bad premonition slammed Nash.

CHAPTER 3

A burly young man ran toward Ela from the parking lot. His intense gaze zeroed in on her, and the closer he came, the more overpowering his height and build seemed. Instinct ordered her to run. But he managed to cut in front of her, and she skidded to a halt.

Drops of water clung to his thin, brown hair, and acne marked his long cheeks. He licked his thin lips. "Excuse me." He gathered the edges of his jean jacket together while hunching his thick shoulders. "I didn't mean to scare you. I belong to SOC. Our group wants the mayor to approve redesigning the town's unsafe roads. We're focused on the Moose Hill curve."

Nothing about him inspired confidence. His worn jeans and his frayed cuffs did little to support his claim as a group's rep.

"You're Ela Danforth?"

"Sorry. I have to go." She started around him.

He jumped in front of her, forcing her to stop, again. "My sister died last year in the spot where your car went over last night. You can help us. You and your sister can join us and force people to listen."

The pepper spray was in her purse. How could she get the tube without letting him know? "I don't even know your name."

"Name is Brown. I left my license in my glove compartment." He angled his jaw toward the lot. "Walk with me to my car. I'll show you my ID." He reached out and snared her wrist.

She fisted her free hand for one good swing at his face.

Tires squealed, and Nash's car sped under the emergency

23

canopy. He swerved to a halt at the curb and jumped out.

"Nash!" she shouted.

His hand went to the small of his back as he sped toward her. The stranger's eyes widened with fear. He turned and fled toward the parking lot.

Nash ignored the man and ran to Ela. "Are you okay?"

She pointed an unsteady finger toward the fleeing figure. "He claimed to be a member of Shoes or Socks. His name is Brown, if you can believe him."

"Sounds fishy. Did he hurt you?"

She shook her head. "He said his sister died on Dead Man's Curve in an accident, and Suz and I should join the protestors for a safer road. Then he grabbed me." She rubbed the spot where she still felt the grip of his steel fingers clenching her skin. In her mind, she saw his grey eyes demanding she do what he wanted.

"Are you sure you're not hurt?" Nash glanced at her massaging her wrist.

She tamped down on her nerves and dropped her arms to her sides. "He rattled me for a second, but I'm fine. I'm sure I could have handled him. Why did you come back?" She threw a glance at the backside of his jacket. "Were you reaching for a gun?" Did he carry one?

"I saw Mr. Brown confront you in my mirror. Come on. We'll report him. And yes, I own a weapon. When you're a lawyer in a small town, you do all kinds of legal business and have to be prepared for a few unsavory characters."

"Doesn't Manhattan own the monopoly on bizarre types?"

"Your city was kind enough to share. Take a second to regroup before we go in the hospital." He took her elbow and guided her onto the grass near the small bushes dotting the side of the building.

No one had made physical contact with her in months, maybe more than a year. The warmth and strength of his touch tempted her to lean into him for support. That was silly. She wasn't desperate for human connections. Yet, memories from the big day when she had longed for someone to be there for her flashed in her mind.

The press had closed around her as she'd approached the courthouse. Inside, the jury would announce her father's fate.

His whole career—his life—hung on the decisions of strangers.

She'd swallowed her fear and scanned the crowd gathered outside the courthouse for a familiar face. Heated expressions glared back at her. People shouted to get her attention. Then they cursed her. She focused on the federal court's double doors and getting inside where she'd be able to breathe.

"Ela?"

The scene in her head faded away, leaving her with Nash. "Yes?"

"Are you okay?"

"What? Oh, sure. I appreciate your gesture, but I can go it alone from here."

"Of course you can, but we should report Mr. Brown or SOC. Two voices are harder to ignore."

Here she was, with a man she'd met only yesterday. *Careful.* The back of her neck tightened with tension but something about the SOC man wasn't right. She should follow Nash's advice.

"When Mr. SOC spoke, he seemed desper—" At the break in her voice, she swallowed to give herself a second to pull it together. "Don't you need to get back to your office, Nash?"

"Don't worry about me. I'm where I should be. Let's take care of Mr. Socks and Shoes. Security sometimes has a list of people to look out for."

"That's reassuring. You mean I can expect more strangers to accost me?"

"Not quite what I meant, but we'll play it safe." They walked through the sliding glass doors. Cool air swirled around them and disappeared within moments. The odor of antibacterial disinfectant hung in the air. Nash paused in the cathedral-ceilinged room with a granite information desk. People passed them with stern expressions, intent on their destinations.

"I recognize the reporter," he murmured under his breath.

She followed his gaze to a short, bald man in baggy pants. He stood in front of the TV on the paneled wall of a waiting area. He was mesmerized by a sports replay on the screen and seemed harmless compared to Mr. SOC.

"We'll call security from upstairs." One of the elevators opened across the hall, and Nash guided Ela forward. He punched a button on the panel.

"I was thinking. I'd like Suz to thank you. It's important. You saved her life."

"I'd be happy to meet her."

"Where are we going?" She raised her gaze to the pane and the lit number.

"I don't know. I was getting us away from the press and just hit the board."

The elevator slowed and jolted to a halt. The doors opened. Ela peeped out. "I hope this isn't the floor with contagious diseases."

"Do you want me to scrounge up a hazmat uniform for you?"

"I'll risk it."

An elderly, round man in a trench coat started into the elevator and paused. He pushed up his steel framed glasses. "Sorry. I thought it was empty." He retreated.

"Not a problem, Pastor, we're getting off."

Pastor? She peered closer and caught the white collar.

"Nash, I didn't recognize you at first. Everyone okay? How are your parents?"

"We're healthy." Nash pushed the button to hold the door. "You doing well?"

"Just visiting the sick. Part of the job. I'll see you again on Sunday. Your mother volunteered the pastries for the coffee chat."

"I'm sure she'll bring your favorite flavor, blueberry." Nash motioned toward her. "This is Ela Danforth."

"I'm pleased to meet you, Miss Danforth." He extended a hand and they exchanged handshakes before she and Nash exited.

The clergyman tapped his fingertips together and walked into the elevator. "Have a good day, both of you. Come by the church, Miss Danforth. We're always open to visitors."

The whine of the elevator's car announced his departure. Ela turned and followed the rainbow painted across an aqua wall to its end in the lobby. Nash walked behind her.

"We must have landed on the maternity or pediatric ward." She paused. "There's a nursery viewing room ahead." Babies.

He glanced toward the other end of the hall. "Let's find the stairs. Ela? Ela?"

She didn't bother to answer. She heard the cry of infants and followed the sounds. When he reached her, she was pressed against the large window. Four newborns tucked in their bassinets slept without a worry in the world. Her arms ached to hold one, inhale their distinct fragrance. "When Suz was born, she looked angelic in her pink cap and blanket."

"They have to look that way or we'd leave them at the hospital." His hazel eyes twinkled.

"What about Lanie? I bet she was irresistible when she was tiny."

"I was deployed to the Mideast and missed her birth. She was five weeks old when I returned. I remember the first time I held her. Cindy put her in my arms, and Lanie stared at me with those newborn baby blues. I told her I was her father, and she smiled. My wife insisted it was gas, but I never believed her. That's when I decided to go to law school and earn a decent paycheck for my family. I'd resisted the call until then." A faraway expression flickered in his eyes for an instant. Then he shifted away from the glass. "I think about that moment with Lanie, a lot when she's misbehaving." The corners of his mouth tilted upward.

"I wasn't prying."

"Of course not, but I will. I'm guessing you don't have children of your own?"

She'd once dreamed of the whole family...and the marriage bit with Aaron, but that could never happen.

"Ela?"

Nash's voice chased away the pain of what might have been real. She raised a hand to her chest trying to ease the hurt although the gesture was useless.

"Sorry if I asked a personal question." He backed away a step.

She shook her head. "Dealing with my sister has temporarily cured me of wanting a child. My parents were ecstatic when Suz arrived." The stress drained from her as she pointed the conversation away from herself. "They'd prayed for another child for years after my birth. I think they'd lost hope."

"Are your parents alive?"

Should she tell him the truth? In his profession, he probably was used to dealing with incarcerated people. But she wanted a few more minutes of normalcy. "My mom's on a permanent vacation from her life. She's traveling in Europe with a best friend. She left after her sister, Aunt Vickie, died. My father isn't around." Ela moved away from the nursery before he could question her further. "Do you have any idea how to get out of here?"

"Let's stop at the nurse's station first and ask about reporting Mr. SOC." Nash led her to the hall desk and spoke with the nurse in charge, who called security.

In minutes, the head of the department, a tall, middle-aged man in a beige uniform appeared, and Nash explained their situation. The security chief promised to fill in the patrol making rounds in the parking lot to be on the alert for a burly, six-foot male from twenty-five to thirty years of age with facial blemishes.

"Does SOC have a permit to block your entrance?" Nash asked him.

The man unclipped a walkie-talkie from his hip. "We're working on moving the protestors to a less intrusive space." He walked away with the device at his lips.

"The morgue would work," Nash said under his breath and turned to face Ela.

"I don't think he'd like your suggestion," she said. "Are you ready for the scary part—meeting my sister?"

"Absolutely. Let's grab the elevator."

Together they crossed the floor and into an open car. The elevator jolted off.

"I bet your sister's happy to meet anyone not wearing a white uniform after the parade of nurses and doctors in her room."

"These days Suz's not happy to see anyone except her boyfriend. She's been different since she hit sixteen. I often wonder who she is." The ding announced they'd reached their floor. "She's at the end of the hall." Ela exited on to the gleaming tiles. The bottom of their shoes squeaked as they walked the sterile corridor. Finally, she slowed at the next to last room.

* * *

She reached for the door, but Nash grabbed the handle and waited for her to enter first. He hoped siszilla wasn't on the other side as he followed Ela into a single-bed room with beige walls and a sparkling white floor. Two windows overlooking the staff parking garage provided light. A blonde teen dressed in a hospital gown sat in the cranked up hospital bed, a cell phone pressed to her ear. She was small in stature like her sister and had the same heart-shaped face. As she spoke, her blue eyes seemed to shoot arrows of anger that would kill anyone who crossed her path.

"Don't worry, Tyler. I'll stand by you. I can't believe they accused you."

"What happened? Are you all right?" Ela hurried to her sister's side.

Her sister shook her head. "You're at home now. Come quick, I can't wait to see you," she gushed into the phone. "I love you. Bye." She dropped the cell phone on the sheet. A tear rolled down her cheek, and she wiped it away with her palm.

Was this his future with Lanie—telling boys she loved them at age sixteen? The idea was enough to make him want to join a monastery.

"What's wrong, Suz?" Ela demanded.

Suz swiped the back of her hand across her eyes and sniffed. "It's Tyler. He's in trouble." Her face hardened. "Did you go to the police and turn him in for something?"

Ela inhaled a breath. "I know you don't want to hear this, but Chief Ballard warned me that your boyfriend hangs out with a rough group, and you should stay away from him."

"I told you he's changed." Suz dug her fingers into the blanket, and the tension thickened in the room. "Last fall, he went to a party, where there was drinking and an expensive antique disappeared from the house. Tyler was a suspect in the theft, along with others when the parents came home and found out what happened. He told me he was innocent, and had no idea anything went missing from the house. The whole episode scared him straight."

Nash cleared his throat. "I'll step outside and let you have some privacy."

"Are you a cop?"

From her tone he knew the girl wasn't complimenting him.

"Nash, you can stay. Of course he's not a cop, Suz. Tyler—"

"Tyler's honest and admitted his problems. He hooked up with the wrong crowd for a while, but not anymore. Since I met him, he goes to school every day, works and then hangs out with me. He was the one person who offered me help the first day of school when I wasn't sure how to find my English class. Everyone else walked past while I wandered around and stared at room numbers. Ela, you can't trust the police. You know that. What else did the useless chief say?"

The girl didn't lack opinions, Nash thought.

Ela tightened her lips and tilted her chin upward. "Chief Ballard asked for permission to analyze the car's ashtray for traces of marijuana."

"What? You let him?"

"I did. He sent the ashes to a lab for diagnosis. He also asked if anyone else besides me or you rode in Aunt Vickie's vehicle."

Nash felt the tension in the room rev up even more—to a courtroom level, but at court, he understood his role.

"You gave him Tyler's name? That's low, Ela. No wonder they asked him all kinds of questions. They think he's a druggie, and they treated him like he sent me over the cliff."

"The police chief was doing his job."

"What if I'm a drug dealer? Did you ever think of that? I was the driver of Aunt Vickie's car, not Tyler."

Ela tensed her shoulders. "Suz, are you selling drugs?"

Nash fastened his gaze on the girl's face, searching for a sign that she was telling the truth.

"If I said yes, you'd say I caused my own accident. I'm getting out of this place." She tossed the blanket aside, revealing one leg in a cast. Suz eased away from the bed, stood and winced. "The seatbelt left bruises on my side." She clutched the edge of the mattress.

"I'll call a nurse," Ela said. "Where's the buzzer?"

"I can step out and get one," Nash offered.

"Hold on a sec." Suz closed her eyes.

Ela hovered by her sister. "Are you okay?"

Suz made a dismissive gesture. "I'm a little dizzy."

"I'm sure the nurse will be glad to help," Nash said, wishing he could be more useful.

Ela studied her sister's face. "You're pale and unsteady. I'm ringing for help."

Suz held up her finger for a second and then nodded. "I'm good to go as soon as I change my clothes."

Nash inched toward the door. "I'm intruding. I'll leave."

Suz jerked her gaze to him. "Who are you?"

"This is Nash McCain, the man who found you after your accident and called the ambulance." Ela threw out a hand toward him. "If he hadn't been around, you might still be at the bottom of Moose Hill and a missing person."

"My name and picture posted on a billboard or TV screen. That would've been a rush."

She waved a hand in the air. "Just kidding. Sort of. Thanks, Nash. Can you give me a hand? I need a little support while I hobble across the floor. The crutches hurt my arms."

"You'll get used to the crutches, and your visitor's name is Mr. McCain," Ela said. "You shouldn't move without a nurse assisting you."

"I called you almost an hour ago. Where've you been?"

Ela hesitated and Nash guessed she was mentally censoring her explanation so as not to worry her sister.

"I was detained," Ela confirmed.

"Your sister braved a crowd to be by your side." Nash crossed the room and steadied Suz.

"Crowd?" Suz wrinkled her nose. "Must be a lot of sick people in this town."

"A protest group blocked the main entrance," he said, "and the news media wants to interview anyone who's crashed on Dead Man's Curve."

"Great." Suz sighed. "No way I'm talking to a bunch of nosey reporters."

"Where to?" he asked. "I'd skip the mountain climbing trip."

"You're a funny guy. My clothes are in the paper bag on the seat." She gestured to the chair against the wall.

At least she was willing to accept his assistance.

"I'll get them." Ela swiped up the brown sack, peeked inside and then opened the bag wider. "These are your clothes. Where did these come from?"

"A friend brought them. The bathroom is straight ahead." Suz limped forward with Nash's arm around her waist.

He moved a step and paused for Suz's next hop. "Your sister is worried about you. She spent hours here last night."

Suz twisted her lips as though about to say something and then glanced at her sister. Finally, she said, "I don't do drugs, El. Neither does Tyler. The results from the ashtray will be negative."

"Thanks for the reassurance, Suz. The police believe your car going off the road might not be an accident. That's why they were asking about drugs. Did you owe money to anyone?"

"Ela, we owe money to everyone." She hopped forward.

They were in debt. Had they moved to Rockypoint to escape payments? "What happened before the crash?" Nash asked.

"I don't remember anything after leaving the driveway. Next thing I know, I find myself in the hospital." She held onto the doorframe of the open bathroom for support. "Mr. Nash, thanks, I got it now. El, can you hand me my clothes?" Suz grabbed the sack from her sister and paused to face him. "I've changed my mind. You look like one of them, but not one of them."

"Who?"

"Ask my sister." She limped over the threshold and shut the door.

Nash raised a brow at Ela.

"She thinks you're a lawyer, which you are." She held her open palms upward and shrugged.

"I was right," Suz yelled from inside the bathroom.

What was going on? "Explain it to me." He tipped his head toward the hall, and they walked out of the room.

"What's the problem with lawyers, and spare me the usual jokes," he said as soon as the door closed.

She looked over his shoulder, avoiding eye contact. "My family's suffered because of the poor advice of our attorneys. I suspect anyone's motives when they belong to the profession. I'm sorry, Mr. McCain. You've been super helpful, but I'll solo from here. I'm capable of handling everything, and I don't want to intrude any longer."

"You want me to leave because I'm a lawyer?" He'd never had a more obvious snub. "For your own protection, hire one. I don't know anyone in the area who's not trustworthy."

"We're fine and don't need legal advice. I'll keep you in mind in case the occasion arises. I should take my sister home, and you mentioned the bank."

A hundred reasons to object burst into his mind. But he had the feeling not one of them would change Ela Danforth's mind. "You know where to find me."

"I do." She hesitated and fiddled with the edge of her coat. "I appreciate your help today, but we should both get on with our business."

"I'll check with security before I leave. If they've found the SOC man, I'll let you know." He marched down the hall fighting the urge to go back and continue the conversation. He ignored it and kept walking toward the exit.

* * *

Ela's phone buzzed and she tore her attention from Nash McCain and shoved away her doubts. Should she or shouldn't she answer the text? It might be one of his messages. She pulled the phone out of her pocket. *Don't read it. He's not worth a second.* Her thumb hovered over the delete.

"Hey, it's the big sister."

Ela's hand tightened around her cell at the familiar greeting, and she trashed the message before she faced the newcomer. "Hello, Tyler."

An invisible cloud of cigarette smoke clung to him and assaulted Ela's nose as he approached. He must have been smoking before he arrived. She inched backward. "You came to visit Suz again?"

"I'm driving her home." He wore his usual bomber outfit. Sunglasses perched on his nose and the hood of his gray sweatshirt pulled up, hiding his profile. He faced her with coiled lips that hinted at an attempted smile.

He resembled an animal baring his teeth. Suz had fallen for his swarthy good looks, but all Ela saw when she looked at him was a young man focused on what he could gobble up for himself.

"She's changing her clothes at the moment. I planned to call a taxi."

"Tyler's Taxi at your service." He pushed the hood off his dark hair and entered the room.

"Sure, go on in," Ela mumbled and followed.

Dressed in blue Capri and a lilac t-shirt, Suz was seated on the cushioned chair against the wall. Her injured leg was stretched out in front of her. "Tyler! At last! Did you get your mom's car or is your truck fixed?"

"Truck's D.O.A. but Mommy came through."

"You're always there for me, Tyler."

He steadied Suz as she rose, and then snapped his attention across the room. "They gave you crutches? Awesome." He trotted away, leaving her to sink into the seat. He snatched up the crutches in the corner. "We should get another pair and race."

"I feel more like Tiny Tim than the Road Runner with those." Suz crossed her arms over her chest. "Can we go? I need your help, Tyler."

"Usually, a nurse checks you out." Ela resisted shaking her head over Tyler's lack of concern. Why wasn't a nurse here?

"I'll help you. Just a minute." He stuffed a crutch under his arm and pivoted around. "I'm a peg leg pirate." His sneakers squeaked against the floor. "Ahoy, Mate. Where's the treasure?"

"Give me those." Ela removed the crutches from his grasp.

The door swung open and a plump, middle-aged nurse rolled a wheelchair into the room. "Someone is going home today." She paused in front of Ela. "You must be the one in charge." She handed Ela a clipboard. "The discharge forms need your signature."

Ela perused them and signed. Her father's health insurance wouldn't cover Suz's hospitalization since he was no longer employed and hadn't paid his coverage for over a year. The measly insurance allotment from her job wouldn't provide much toward the hospital bill. She'd better hurry and sell the antiques in Aunt Vickie's store and house. Of course, Ela wouldn't mention her plan to Suz. Her sister would share the idea with Tyler, and who knew what he'd dream up? He'd already asked the worth of the vase in their front entry with a calculated gleam in his eyes.

When Ela gave the nurse the signed papers, Suz was already in the wheelchair, and Tyler was holding the plastic water pitcher and cup. "Are these on your bill?"

"Part of the tab," the nurse said.

"Aunt Vickie owns a dozen pitchers and glasses," Ela interjected. "We're set."

"I'll take them for our new apartment." He dropped the cup inside the pitcher and tucked it under his arm. "Let's see how fast that buggy can go." He grinned at Suz.

"The hospital speed limit is slow." The gray-haired nurse took control of the wheelchair and pushed Suz toward the exit.

Tyler darted in front of them. "Ladies." He swung the door open for the nurse and was on the verge of going through when he caught Ela staring at him. "After you."

The last thing she wanted was to have her back to Tyler, although she had no concrete reason to distrust him. To be safe, she tossed a glance at him over her shoulder as she exited.

They rode in silence on the elevator. The possibility Tyler had driven the pickup that forced Suz to crash wouldn't leave her thoughts. But what would he gain from hurting his girlfriend? Nothing. She should relax. The elevator lowered to a stop and they went out the door without incident.

Tyler busied himself with assisting Suz into the front seat of a dented gold compact. Ela strapped herself into the torn rear seat and began again to regret sending away Nash McCain. His decisive actions and easy manner inspired confidence. With his personality, Nash must have a ton of clients, and women lined up to date him.

The compact's engine rattled to life. The traffic was brisk. At least Tyler couldn't drive too fast on the busy street. In a few minutes, they'd be home.

At the end of Hospital Way, he hung a left. "What are you doing?" Ela edged forward and strained against the seatbelt. "You're going in the wrong direction."

He met her gaze in the rearview mirror. "We're going to Dead Man's Curve."

"Tyler says returning to the scene of the accident will help me remember," Suz replied from her front seat.

Remember what? If they got to the curve and Suz suddenly recalled it was *Tyler's* truck that forced her off the road, would he finish the job? Sucking in a shallow breath, Ela fought the premonition spinning in her head. Was another accident about to happen?

CHAPTER 4

After Ela expressed her belief that visiting the accident scene would be unproductive and the teens ignored her, she closed her eyes and held onto her seatbelt. For a decade old car with rust spots, the engine powered along. Where was a speed trap when you wanted one? It was an officer's duty to protect the public.

She should have accepted Nash's ride. A pang of regret tugged at her conscience. She'd been short with him. She should have tried harder to make him understand.

Ela repressed a sigh. When was the last time she felt safe and happy? One particular Sunday floated into her mind. The maitre d' had led them to a white-linen covered table at Dad's favorite Big Apple restaurant and advised them of the specials while he handed them their menus. The waiter filled the water glasses.

Her father and mother perused the list of foods, and Ela breathed in the spicy aroma lingering in the air. Next to her, Suz giggled over a joke Aaron told her. She was always giggling in those days.

Two violinists appeared by their table to serenade them. "I have something to keep a smile on everyone's face. I hope." Aaron produced a small, black box from his pocket and held it out to Ela.

Her chest swelled with surprise.

The motion of the car stopping drew her attention into the present. Tyler hopped out first, followed by Suz and herself. Ela hugged her arms to her chest and hovered near the compact. The last place she'd dreamed she'd be today was on Dead Man's Curve with her sister and her possibly nefarious boyfriend.

A raw breeze whipped strands of hair into her face, and the gray sky threatened more rain. In the distance, the White Mountains rose up and guarded the entry to their forest. Shoving away the stray pieces of hair, she said, "Don't go close to the edge, Suz. The side might be slippery."

"I want to see where I went over." Suz accepted the crutches from Tyler, and step by step, they proceeded toward the slope.

How had they gotten into this crazy situation? If Aaron were here, he'd have negotiated their way out of it. From his father, the Judge, he'd inherited the ability to analyze a social scene; from his brother, Ray the mediator, he'd learned to arbitrate. The legal eagle triumvirate, Aaron had referred to the men in his family. *Someday, the three of us will work together*, he'd said. His dream changed after Ela's father offered him a place with their firm. It had all changed because of *her*.

"Come on." Tyler's voice interrupted her musings. He broke away to stride ahead to the bend and left Suz hobbling beside Ela. "Wow, you crushed the metal guardrail where you spun out. You were flying." He paced to the dirt shoulder and paused near the damaged section of rail. "I wish I'd seen the accident."

Suz and Ela joined him on the curve. In the distance, the Rockypoint houses looked liked dollhouse furniture. Suz's wary expression drew Ela closer to her sister.

Suz straightened quickly. "I don't remember anything." But her face grew even paler and she backed toward the pavement.

"You have to give it more than a glance." Tyler balanced on the periphery and threw out his hands to the slope below. "It's a big drop."

Ela's microscopic trust in him grew smaller by the minute. She moved to his side. "I'll fill in for my sister." She inched forward, keeping a few feet between herself and Tyler, and glanced lower. Rocks and brush protruded from the hill.

"Try hard to remember, Suz," he said. "You can do it."

Suz approached the border again and stood between them.

"I bet you flew off and landed there." Tyler pointed to an upturned patch of fresh earth and rocks scattered across the ground about three hundred feet from the road. "Then you flipped over and over to where you landed against those trees." Deep gashes marred the trunks. "Crash, bam, whack!" His face glowed with each sound effect.

Ela visualized Aunt Vickie's car suspended in the air for a fraction of a minute before dropping to the earth and somersaulting down the hill. The sound of metal hitting against the rocks echoed in her mind until the vehicle smashed against the trees.

She jerked her gaze to Suz. "You should be thankful you're alive." An urge to whisper a prayer of thanks seized her, but why waste words that went unheard? She shook off the idea.

Her sister's lower lip quivered.

"Boo!" Tyler grabbed Suz's shoulders.

She shrieked.

He laughed. "Scared ya."

"I've had enough. Suz, are you coming?" Ela asked, ready to sprint away.

"Hold up," Tyler ordered, stretching his body over for another glimpse. "I bet the EMTs trampled the bushes around the smashed car to get to you. See the pile of broken branches lying on the ground. Man, how cool was it when they used the Jaws of Life? I missed everything."

"I want to go home," Suz whispered leaning on her crutches. "I'm ready, El."

A gust of wind blew dirt and sticks at them while Ela crept along with her sister. A truck roared up the road and shot past them. On the shoulder, Tyler snapped pictures with his phone. Then he strolled toward them and pocketed his cell while Ela assisted Suz into the front seat and stuffed the crutches in the rear.

He hopped inside. "I've got a few good shots to post on Facebook. Suz, you can use them for evidence to sue and make the big bucks. You should wear one of those collars around your neck to impress a jury. I bet they'd give you lots of money. You'd be rich." He started the engine and the car roared off onto the road.

"We'd have enough to rent an apartment," Suz's voice rose with enthusiasm, and Ella fought a cringe.

She couldn't wait to be inside her house, safe and far away from Moose Hill. Tyler must have exhausted his quota of schemes for the day. She cracked the window and concentrated on the fresh air.

They reached the residential downtown. Tyler slowed to the speed limit. "Hey, Sis, know a good lawyer who'd help us in court?" He stared at her in the rearview mirror.

First, she wasn't his sis, but since he was driving, it didn't seem the perfect moment to voice her disagreement.

"We don't like lawyers," Suz interjected, "except for the one who helped me yesterday."

"I bet they have a Dummies book about going to court." Tyler laughed. "Forget the apartment. We'll buy a mansion. I bet we score an easy million."

Suz shifted within the confines of her seatbelt to speak over the front seat to Ela. "You should talk to that Nash guy, El. He'd represent us."

"Who's he again?" Tyler asked.

"He was the one who found me when I crashed. He visited me at the hospital this morning. Ela, you should ask him for advice. He has a thing for you." Suz threw Ela a knowing smile. "He kept staring at you."

A flush of pleasure went through her. Then she got a grip on her emotions. "I'm not sure *a thing* is flattering."

"Does he drive a green sports car?" Tyler asked.

"How did you know?" Had Tyler spied on her?

"The guy's following us." Tyler hooked a thumb over his shoulder.

Ela turned in her seat. The lime-green sports coupé was following a car's length behind. Why was Nash tailing them?

"I can lose him," Tyler offered.

Ela pictured them swerving through alleys and dodging pedestrians on street corners. "No, don't bother. We're only two blocks from home."

The image of Nash McCain in his office popped into her head. The hunky man stood over his desk in his rolled up shirtsleeves with her present in his hands. His figure faded and sharpened into Aaron holding out the engagement ring, a silver band with an enormous solitary diamond.

Emotional pain jabbed her, and she slammed down on the memories as they turned into the driveway with Nash behind them. Once Tyler cut the engine, Ela jumped out and marched to Nash's car, which he was now standing beside. "There was no need to tail us, Mr. McCain. I don't want legal advice."

"You left your umbrella in my car." He reached behind the two seats and pulled out the black umbrella. "The forecast predicts rain," His earnest voice and the one shock of brown hair falling over his forehead added to his generous gesture.

"Thank you," she said, lowering her voice. Embarrassment crawled up her neck. "I finished my banking and came by to drop it off, but you weren't home. I was on my way to the office when I passed you, so I turned around."

"You were very thoughtful." What was wrong with her, yelling at him in the driveway? He wasn't a stalker. How could she make amends? "Do you want to come inside? I can put on the coffee."

"I'll take a rain check. I've a meeting with an important client."

She clutched the umbrella to her chest. A bigger fool didn't exist. What could she say to the man who'd worried she'd get wet? "Thanks."

A few feet away, Tyler and Suz gawked at them.

"Anytime. Is everything okay with your sister and her boyfriend?" He threw a quizzical glance their way.

"They're teenagers." She swatted her hand in the air to dismiss his concern.

"I'd better go. The boss will be looking for me." After nodding to Suz and Tyler, he climbed into the driver's seat and reversed out onto the street.

She gave a small wave as he left and caught the movement of the window curtain dropping in the house across the street. Her neighbor was enjoying the action.

"He brought my umbrella," she mumbled to Tyler and Suz, even though they'd observed the exchange. She left Tyler to assist her sister. The familiar sight of the house was a welcome relief. In a few minutes, she'd enjoy peace and sanity in her own little world, a place she could control. Suz and Tyler's voices rose, and snatches of their conversation floated through the cool, spring air.

Ela unlocked the front door and stepped into the maize-colored hall. The front closet was wide open and hid the Chinese vase and the antique gait-leg table. Strange. It was never left open.

"Hello?" A knot formed in her stomach as she peeked into the room Aunt Vickie called her parlor. She sent a searching glance over the contents of the crowded space: the Morris recliner, the crimson settee beside the Tiffany floor lamp and the fireplace— Wait a minute. A plate with a half-eaten sandwich sat on the tea table near the hearth.

The front door banged shut. Suz swung into the house on her crutches with Tyler. "Ela, what's wrong?"

"Someone's been in the house. We need to leave. I'll call the police." She dug out her phone from her pocket and waved them toward the door.

Tyler shifted his gaze from Ela to Suz. "Is your sister paranoid or something?"

"Someone broke in while I was gone. He left part of his sandwich. He could still be in here hiding." Ela fished in her other pocket until her hand closed over the pepper spray she'd moved from her purse for faster access.

Tyler stayed put. "I know who it was."

Ela halted on the edge of the flowered wool rug. "Who?"

He shoved his hands into his pockets. "Me."

"How'd you get in?"

He swapped another glance with Suz.

She let out an exasperated sigh. "I gave him a key. He was getting my clothes. I didn't tell you because you'd twist it into a major crime."

He'd driven over for Suz's outfit and stopped to make and eat some of a sandwich? Ela set her cell on the coffee table and crossed the carpet. She blocked his view of the food. "What kind of sandwich were you eating?"

"Are you testing me?" He fisted his hand by his side and then relaxed it. "I made a peanut butter, my usual."

She glanced over her shoulder and spotted the brown spread between the slices. She rubbed the muscles pulling at the back of her neck. "I'm sorry, Tyler. I guess I overreacted." She paused and added, "Our visit to Moose Hill left me...unsettled. Now I can picture someone forcing Suz off the road, and Aunt Vickie's car tumbling down the hill."

"Yeah, about her accident." Tyler walked over to the table by the hearth, raised the leftover food and bit into it.

The slices had to be stale. "What about it?"

Suz swung closer on her crutches. "Tyler doesn't think anyone tried to kill or knock me off the road on purpose. Lots of kids race up the hill. They try to beat each other's records. It's a cool contest."

Ela stared. "Suz, were you racing?"

"Me?" She widened her eyes and shook her head. "I didn't know they held races until Tyler told me. Ela, no one broke in. No one wanted to hurt me."

"She's right," Tyler said. "Kids meet at the hill and challenge each other lots of nights."

"Ela," Suz interjected. "The kid driving probably recognized me from school and thought I was up for a little contest. You can relax. We live in Rockypoint where the kids hang out and try to beat each other's times on a big hill. That's the thrill in town."

Was her sister right? Ela crossed into the hall. The open door bothered her. Why had Tyler opened the coat closet if he'd come for Suz's jeans and shirt? He'd been in the house enough times to know Suz's clothes were in her bedroom.

Ela had closed the closet herself this morning. She twisted the dead bolt on the main door before she returned to the parlor.

She paused in front of Tyler sitting on the settee with Suz. "Did you get something besides food and Suz's clothes when you came earlier?"

"No, why?"

"Nothing." She needed to think. She turned on her heel to go to the kitchen.

"If you decide to cook, don't forget I love macaroni," he called after her.

"I'll let the chef know when I find him."

She walked past the mahogany dining room set and pushed through the swinging door. In the kitchen, the modern stove disguised as an old-fashioned cook stove sat near the closeted stainless steel refrigerator with no signs of anyone touching either. The glass-fronted cupboards showed no evidence of disturbance. Nothing seemed out of place. She sank into a chair, rested her arms on the ivory tablecloth and allowed the quiet to seep into her. Inhaling the familiar scent of the rose scented geranium on the sill over the porcelain sink, she relaxed.

"Ela!" Suz screamed. "Come quick."

She ran back to Tyler and Suz hovered near the fireplace.

"Is something wrong with your leg?" Ela searched her sister, leaning on one crutch, for signs of swelling or new bruising.

"It's Mom. Someone cut up her picture." With an unsteady hand, Suz held up the oval white picture frame they kept on the mantle.

The photo of their mother was now headless. Ela stared at the picture. Sure enough, Mom's face no longer smiled at them.

"I saw it when we sat on the sofa," Suz said.

Tyler pointed at the photo. "Someone didn't care for the headshot."

"Did you notice the picture was destroyed when you came earlier?" Ela demanded of him.

"I never noticed it. I was thinking a snack would be good."

"I'm calling Chief Ballard." Ela went into the kitchen to speak to him in private. Tears of anger burned in her eyes and throat. Rockypoint was supposed to be different. She'd promised Suz. It was starting to feel like New York all over again.

Ela dragged out a chair from under the table and plopped into it. She drew her cell from her pocket. The card with Nash McCain's phone number written in bold print slipped out with her phone. She fingered it while she pushed in Chief Ballard's digits.

* * *

Money Bags was doing his I'm-the-King act. If he didn't need the cash, he'd tell him where to go in two words.

"What's taking so long?" Money demanded. "Answer me. Are you too dumb to speak?"

"I'm having a little fun. You should have seen them running around in the house when they found the pictu—"

"You want to play, go to a playground," Money growled. "Do your job, or I'll find someone else."

"Hey, don't rush me. I can do my job without you telling me what to do every two minutes. I don't do well with pressure. You want it done right or messy?" He rubbed the back of his neck.

"Just do it, now," Money ordered. "Stop wasting time." The phone clicked off.

Money thought he could boss him around. He'd show him.

CHAPTER 5

Yesterday had been another day without answers from Chief Ballard. Would they ever discover the truth about the accident? In the past, Ela had prayed harder than anyone for solutions and gotten nothing except heartbreak. She'd lost her home, her father and her fiancé, Aaron. Never mind the fact her friends had treated her like she'd joined a terrorist group.

She wouldn't waste her time again trying to understand the tragedies in her life. At least their mother was safe, reliving her youth with an old roommate from college, though she seemed to have forgotten her daughters.

Ela crumpled a napkin and tossed it on the kitchen tablecloth. From the counter came the ring of her phone. She rose and checked the caller ID. It was *him*. Okay, she was tired of his game and changing her number. She hit the talk button.

"The wicked are estranged from the womb. They go astray and are punished as soon as—"

Bolstered by anger, she enunciated each word, "Don't-ever-call-me-again." She hit the end button.

* * *

"I'll be honest." Nash McCain swiveled his office chair toward his father and law partner seated on the other side of the desk. "I recommend settling. Jurors won't want to award Harrington anything for his whiplash once everyone hears how belligerent he acted toward the police. Even his body language is hostile."

"I agree. A settlement is the best option, but convincing him is another job." His dad's white hair, trim physique and calm approach made him a favorite among his peers.

"Joanne reported that while I was out of the office, the media interviewed you about the girl who crashed on Moose Hill. Are you going to let your mother know about the piece before she watches it on tonight's news?"

"I spoke to Mom. When I hung up, she was still trying to talk me into a hero dinner."

"She called me," his dad said. "I wanted to warn you, she asked a lot of questions about the crash victim's single sister."

"I'm sure 'single' was the key word. We should hire her to investigate for us."

"I can't afford her. Can you imagine what she'd negotiate for pay?"

Dad was a fierce opponent at the courthouse but an easy touch when it came to his wife.

"How about the possibility a case will result from the Moose Hill accident?"

Ela Danforth's image appeared in Nash's mind. Her chestnut hair fell in a mass of curls to her shoulders, and her large, brown eyes that avoided his gaze hid secrets he'd love to unearth.

Nash shut down the memory and redirected his attention to his father. "Sorry, Dad, no new business there."

"Keep the crash on your radar, just in case."

Ela had made it clear she wasn't interested in his services, or any lawyer's, never mind a more-than-business relationship. Despite his initial reservations, he might consider more than a work liaison with this woman.

"Providence strikes when you least expect it, or as your mother believes, 'God works in mysterious, profitable ways.'"

"Mom's an optimist, and I wouldn't dare question her version of the quote." Nash closed the Harrington file on his desktop. If he trusted his mother's beliefs, Ela should reappear in his life.

His secretary buzzed. "Miss Danforth is on your line."

Mother strikes again. Nash picked up his phone.

* * *

The rainclouds disappeared the next day, and the sun peeked out. Ela was about to leave for the appointment she'd made yesterday with Nash McCain. She walked into the parlor. Where on earth was her sister?

"Ela!"Suz shouted from another room.

Ela raced through the house and into Aunt Vickie's office next to the kitchen. "What is it? Are you hurt?"

"I found family pictures." Suz was seated in the maroon leather chair. Her crutches leaned against a paneled wall covered by shelves of books. She held up a brown album.

Ela leaned against the doorframe, her pulse racing. "After Mom's chopped figure and the trip to the scene of your accident, I don't need shouting."

"Sorry." Suz lowered the album. "Calling the cops yesterday was a waste. All they did was cause trouble for Tyler and snoop around our house."

Ela tapped her foot on the floor and folded her arms over her chest. "Suz, did you scream for a specific reason?"

"You have to look at these pictures of Aunt Vickie and Mom." She flipped through the pages. "They're laughing in all of them."

Ella's interest sharpened. "Where did you find them?"

"The album was in the bottom desk drawer. I was trying to find a pen, though Aunt Vickie probably used a feather and ink well." Suz raised the open page. "Can you believe it? There's Mom with her hair messed up. She always worried if one piece was out of place. I should label this Mom Gone Wild."

Underneath the plastic protector, her mother's hair was big and curly. Aunt Vickie wore a ponytail with a few curly strands escaped to frame her heart-shaped face. Both women were dressed in jeans and v-necked sweaters. The lens caught them in mid-laughter with their mouths open. Their lips curved upward.

"Aunt Vickie saved lots of pictures. Here's one where they're sitting on the porch. It's the same furniture that's on it now, and the house was painted the identical pink with purple trim." Suz gestured to the snapshot. "I'm going to take a picture of Mom for my room. When she comes home, I'll show her. Maybe I'll email it to her."

"Good idea." At least her sister had calmed down. Ela

wouldn't have blamed her if she hadn't. No clues pointed to the identity of the trespasser who'd invaded their home and decapitated their mother's photo.

Suz slipped a picture out of the plastic. "I wish I'd known Aunt Vickie better. We always spent more time with Dad's family because they lived in the city. If she'd had children, we'd never have inherited the house."

"I'm sure she'd appreciate your sentiments. I think we should paint the house a more neutral, less attention grabbing color."

Suz spun toward her in the office chair. "I like it. The color's grown on me."

Ela waited for her sister to add, "like fungus," but she remained silent. Ela could never predict Suz's reactions. Her emotions were up and down. Ela had hoped the move would help Suz find stability. "I'll leave the paint decision to you. If you want the pink and lilac to stay, it will."

Her sister beamed. She rested the album on her lap and ran a fingertip over her mother's profile. "I miss Mom, El."

An ache settled in the middle of Ela's stomach and threatened to spread. "I do too. She's glad we inherited the old place." Ela cleared her throat. "We should frame more pictures from the album. We won't let a crazy person prevent us from displaying our snapshots. This is a Danforth house, and we're Danforth women."

"Right on, Sistah!" Suz fisted her hand in the air. "Aunt Vickie stored a box of frames in the attic. I'll get a new one for the mantle." She collected the sympathy cards that littered the top of the desk and stuffed them in a drawer.

"Do me a favor. Don't scream when you find one." Ela started to leave and paused. "I'm going to an appointment with Mr. McCain in a few minutes. Keep the doors locked, and don't let anyone inside while I'm gone."

"Yeah, yeah, don't worry. Tyler's at school. I told him I'd be recovered and back tomorrow." Suz stood. "Why are you talking to Mr. McCain? I thought you weren't interested in him."

Ela didn't want to alert Suz to her real reason. Her sister had enough drama in her life. "I might sell a few of Aunt Vickie's pieces, and I need advice from someone who knows the best places for resale."

"I bet he'll charge a huge consultation price. You should sell on eBay." Suz pointed to the album on the desktop. "Dad's photo is inside. You don't think he was sorry when he apologized at his trial, do you?"

"Dad had other motivators." Ela opened her mouth to explain further when she caught Suz's deep sigh.

"You mean he told white lies so people wouldn't be mad at him," Suz said.

"Sometimes an apology or white lies, no matter how well intentioned, can't repair the damage. Actions have consequences."

"He could have been sorry because he loved us and wanted to save us from everybody's anger?"

The soft plea in her sister's voice caused Ela's heart to lurch. She softened her own. "Suz, Dad cheated and harmed a lot of people."

"What about Aaron?"

Aaron…they were going to be the model married couple. She tamped down on the ache near her heart. The image that she'd struggled to erase from her mind shot into her thoughts. Exhausted and desperate, Aaron struggled in the water to stay afloat in the sea.

"El?"

Ela's throat constricted, and she wiped a hand over her face before facing Suz.

"Don't you miss him?" Suz's lip quivered.

"He's not here." He was in a watery grave, wasn't he? Yes, now nothing could hurt him, she told herself to end the nausea and doubts.

"Yeah, but don't his parents, Ellen and the Judge, write you? What about his brother Ray? Doesn't he call and ask how you're doing? Doesn't that make you sad?"

"I haven't seen them in months," she said easily, as though she was referring to a pair of lost socks. She glanced at her watch to end the conversation. "I have to go, Suz."

Ela walked back into the parlor and scooped up the furniture inventory she was creating for the sale. The paper shook in her hand. Suz's questions had aroused a myriad of feelings. *Get it together. Stop letting the past upset you.*

She climbed the stairs to the second floor where she filed the list in her bedroom dresser. She threw a glance toward the mirror. Her face was flushed, betraying her emotions. The cool air outside would help. By the time she walked to McCain's law firm, she could blame the nip in the spring air for her color. Ela changed into a white tailored blouse and beige pants. She missed being able to wear her city clothes, but they seemed too formal in Rockypoint. She was meeting Nash McCain for a quick briefing on security. She focused on the man. Thinking of him brought no pain.

He'd charged to her rescue when Mr. SOC had grabbed her. Who wouldn't feel a flutter of attraction for a man who'd pulled the Sir Galahad act? But there was more. He'd insisted on helping her avoid the press at the hospital, and finally, he was the man who'd driven out of his way because he hadn't wanted her to get wet in the rain.

She'd never met anyone like him. But then, she was in Rockypoint. She'd fallen through a time tunnel into another place, a place where she hadn't found her niche, and Nash McCain seemed surreal. He probably saw a lawsuit and dollar signs from her sister's accident whenever they met. The publicity from the case would be huge in this small community. That and another man who pretended to be strong just for her were the last things she wanted.

She ran down the stairs. In the hall, she shrugged into her jacket and grabbed her purse.

As she opened the door, Nash McCain's sports car turned into her driveway. What timing. She caught herself smoothing her unruly hair before stepping outside.

He waved and smiled his grin that radiated charm.

Her heart did a spin in her chest, and the pleasure jolted her into reality. She'd sworn off men and moved miles and miles only to run into a man to die for. She shook her head and strode toward him. "Mr. McCain, I never expected you to drive to my house. I was on my way to your office."

"I thought I'd save you the walk," he said, climbing out of his car.

She studied him for flaws as he drew closer. His hair was a little too long, and he wore a gray suit that set him apart from the casual dress of the majority of Rockypoint's inhabitants. In New York, he would have blended in on the street. Almost. His unhurried long stride and the perpetual light in his eyes that teased he had a joke you'd die to know, marked him as different.

"Are you all right?" His gaze flickered over her face while his brow creased with concern.

"Sure." She glanced back at the house, hoping Suz wasn't peering out at them. No sign of her. She must be too involved in her picture frame search. "If you don't mind, why don't we take a stroll through the neighborhood? My sister is inside, and I'd rather not discuss our situation within earshot of her."

"I'm all yours. Which way?" He raised his brows.

"Aunt Vickie always told us to walk on the sunny side of the street." That sounded dumb. If only she could rewind and replay her answer with a different comeback.

"Aunt Vickie must have been a wise woman."

He was too good to be true, she reminded herself. They started off through the neighborhood of Victorians dotted with ranch and Cape Cod style homes. Several of the yards boasted yellow and purple crocuses. A squirrel scurried by and raced up one of the oak trees that lined the sidewalks. A few cars passed by at a leisurely speed. With the hustle of getting to work and school runs finished, calm had settled over the neighborhood.

"Is it safe to talk now, or does your sister possess a super-hearing power?" he asked, halfway down the block.

"I wouldn't be surprised. I was trying to figure out where I should start." She raised a hand when he opened his mouth to interrupt. "The beginning, I know." She locked her fingers together at her waist. "When we arrived home yesterday from the hospital, Suz discovered someone had cut off our mother's head in the photo on the mantel." She rushed onward. "I went through the rest of the house and found nothing else touched or missing."

He halted abruptly. "Did you call the police?"

"I did. Two officers on patrol came over, and Chief Ballard dropped in to take notes. The officers searched the house and found an open window in the kitchen. Someone must have entered through it."

"I'm not sure I'd bet on Ballard's theory. Who do you suspect?"

Something was going on between these two men, she thought, but she had bigger problems. Now he'd learn the truth about her. She was paranoid.

"I suspect everyone." A mutilated picture was scary, and the idea that someone had snuck into our house to destroy personal property was creepier. "Suz was upset, too. Usually she accuses me of overreacting, but she was subdued last night. She's back to her normal self today."

Nash strolled forward with her. "Her boyfriend seems a little...out there. Was he around when you found the mutilated picture?"

"Tyler was with us. I don't trust him either, but Suz swears he's a good person. I'm trying to be fair. My sister usually isn't wrong about people. But, I worry she's desperate for a friend and blind to the truth. Do you know his family, the Rawlings?"

"I don't know much. They moved to Rockypoint a few years ago. The father runs a garage on the outskirts of town. He's a decent mechanic."

She shrugged her shoulders. "Have you heard of any sickos who break into houses and cut up family pictures?"

"Not that I recall. You've had a lot of strange things happen lately. Have you had similar incidents in the past?"

She might as well get it out in the open. She moistened her lips. "My father was a financial advisor who gave a lot of bad advice in exchange for his fees. Maybe you'll recognize his name, Matt Blanchette."

He blinked and then his jaw dropped. "Matt Blanchette, the financial advisor whose trial was broadcast on TV?"

"That's the one, and yes, Suz and I changed our last names." She swallowed the lump of misery. "Weren't you glued to the court drama? Lots of people signed up for an email to let them know when the verdict was reached."

"I didn't have time to watch or email. My father and I were involved in a huge lawsuit at the time, but I remember his arrest was big news."

"My father was infamous, at least, during his court appearances. I was his partner in the firm and people labeled me guilty by association. Most of his former clients demanded their money or our blood as payback." She rubbed at the ache in her forehead. "We couldn't give them either. Once, I expected my father's face to appear on a magazine cover as Businessman of the Year. Instead, he was plastered on every tabloid as Crook of the Year."

He let out a whistle. "I'm sorry, Ela, for all your problems. Could one or more of your clients have been mad enough to follow you to Rockypoint?"

"They were too broke to follow us. But more than one threatened us. We kept the police busy. The detectives in New York interviewed and ran background checks on everyone suspicious, but nothing happened to these people. A few took every opportunity to harass us." Resentment roughened her voice.

"I understand you're angry. I apologize if I'm speaking out of line, but you're in Rockypoint now. Prayers and help from others have gotten me over the rough spots and can do the same for you."

She stopped, uneasy with his last words. "I've lost almost everyone I loved, even when I prayed or sought a kind word from friends or strangers. My fiancé Aaron Wright and I were both under investigation, and no one offered a word of support." Once the news about her father's arrest broke, people stopped answering her calls or texts. She was uninvited to parties and told she was unwelcome in the homes of those who once claimed to enjoy her company.

"Sometimes we need the strength of someone stronger than ourselves, Ela. And when we recover, we pay it forward."

What did he, a well-to-do lawyer in a small city, know about challenges or her life before now? "When my father was taken into custody, everyone turned away from me and pretended not to know me, never mind support me."

"Maybe you were in the wrong place. You're not alone now. And remember, if we keep faith, we're never alone."

She inhaled to compose herself. No sense in arguing with him. His firm voice alerted her to the strength of his convictions. "You can believe what you want, but I hope you'll respect my feelings."

"I understand, and we all deal with adversity in different ways, but think about what I've said."

She resumed walking. All this type of talk did was spotlight how alone and different she was. Nash didn't understand.

"Do you mind me asking what happened to your fiancé?"

"Aaron became enmeshed in the fallout from my father's crimes, which he didn't deserve. He went missing at sea before he was indicted, and I can't make it up to him." She caught Nash's surprised expression. "My primary worry is for Suz," she said, changing the topic and easing her own pain. She motioned for them to head back.

Once they u-turned, she resumed talking. "My sister's an easy target. She reacts in the moment and gives little thought to consequences."

She paused again to face him. "I wanted to speak to you for two reasons. First, I want to apologize for my rudeness the other day. You were kind and I wasn't." She waved aside his objection. "Next, I have a simple request" She didn't want him thinking she was creating reasons for them to get together.

"Shoot. I'm listening."

"I found Aunt Vickie's security cameras at her store. They're ancient, but they work. Can you recommend a handyman who'd install them at my home at a reasonable price?" She resumed strolling and slid him a sideways glance.

"I'll do the job."

"Super. What are your rates, Mr. McCain?"

"For you, my preferred fudge maker, the special free price." His eyes twinkled with that mischievous glint.

A pinprick of pleasure followed by dismay rushed through her. What would he want in return? No one did something for nothing, no matter where they lived. "I can't accept charity."

"Who mentioned a handout? Another box of fudge, or a dinner, and you're paid in full." He glanced at his watch. "I'm sorry. One of my clients asked me to squeeze him in. I have to go, but I'll get back to you about the setup."

Had he mentioned dinner? She should say something to clarify her feelings. She waited until they reached her driveway so she could have the final word. "Thanks for your offer. Let me know what I'll owe in cash."

"We'll work it out." He flashed a killer grin, drawing her closer, holding her fascinated.

His strong mouth curved upward. His lips parted and then he moved slightly forward as though he was about to whisper words meant just for her.

The blare of a defective muffler's blast on the street brought her back to reality.

What was wrong with her? A handsome man smiled at her, and she almost jumped into his arms. How had she been reduced to this? She inched away, seeking distance between them. "I hope you take personal checks," she answered in her coolest voice and left him near his car.

The next day, work at the library proved a challenge. Ela's cart of books to shelve piled up often during the day, while her mind replayed yesterday's meeting with Nash. She examined his words and gestures for hidden meanings. By the time she was on her way home, she still hadn't banished him from her thoughts. She began to run the list of Aunt Vickie's items to sell through her mind to blot out Mr. McCain.

A block from the house, the hum of an engine hooked her attention. She glanced over her shoulder. A sleek, navy, four-door sedan crept near the curb, a few feet behind her. Was it following her? She increased her pace, dug out her pepper spray and palmed it in her fist.

The car continued to glide along.

She swerved to the right and darted glances around the neighborhood. A dog tied on a porch barked at her. Otherwise, no one was around.

She broke into a lope and tossed a glance at her pursuer. The car swerved to the curb in front of the green two story with the for sale sign in the yard.

Relief expanded in her chest. Her imagination was running away with her. Her cell rang. She kept an eye on the parked vehicle and dug out the phone to see Chief Ballard's ID.

The sedan pulled into the house's driveway, reversed back into the street and then took off in the opposite direction. She was being paranoid.

"Hello, Chief?"

"I put in a rush for the ashtray results, and they're back. The tests showed cigarette residue, nothing else."

She relaxed her grip on the phone. "Do you have anything more for me?"

"I've nothing to report on the photo episode. We're canvassing the Moose Hill area, and going through the registrations of white trucks in and around Rockypoint. That's all I have at the moment. I'll let you know when we get a break, but the hill seems to be a challenge the high school kids can't resist. Chances are good your sister got caught up in what seemed like a little harmless fun. Kids don't think about the dangers of speed. I'm increasing the patrol in that section of the road."

Suz had told her the truth. She didn't use drugs. Ela dropped the phone into her purse and picked up her pace. Aunt Vickie's pink house along with a green sports car sitting in the drive came into view. Why was Nash McCain, the man she was trying to forget, at her home? She hurried forward to find out.

Suz sat in a wicker chair on the porch with the crutches propped against the clapboard wall. Her voice carried across the lawn to Ela. Although she couldn't catch the gist of the conversation, her sister's animated tone suggested Suz was enjoying her visit with the lawyer. He was resting his hip on the railing and appeared to be listening.

"Here she comes," Suz said to Nash as Ela marched up the steps.

He turned and raised his glass of lemonade to her.

"Nash, I didn't expect to see you today." At least he couldn't hear her heart pounding away.

"Don't blame your sister for letting me stay. I insisted."

"He came to install Aunt Vickie's cameras, and I didn't invite him into the house because you weren't home. So he can stay?"

Ela sighed. "It appears I'm outnumbered."

"And, he's not dangerous, even though he did offer me a bribe." Suz's face brightened on the last word.

Ela lifted her brows. "How'd you bribe her?"

"I ordered pizza to be delivered in an hour, for supper."

"What kind did you order?" Suz asked. "The *Pizza Man Can* makes the best. My boyfriend works there."

"Suz! Mr. McCain was generous to think of us."

"Pepperoni, and it's not hard to think about two beautiful women," Nash answered.

"You sound like a lawyer, but good job ordering." Suz gave him a thumbs up.

That was her sister, easy to impress. Of course, Ela shouldn't judge. She'd tried to entice Nash with a box of fudge. "We've lots of food in the freezer. The neighbors and my coworkers dropped off plenty after our aunt's funeral. You should cancel your order, and I can send you home with a small feast."

"El, we love pepperoni. I don't want another casserole."

Nash inched toward Ela. "If I cancel at the last moment, I'll still have to pay, and I love pepperoni, too."

"Ela, you can't make him pay for uneaten food."

She seemed to get deeper in his debt every day. She shook her head in surrender. "Suz is right, and I owe you a supper in exchange for putting in the cameras."

He clapped his hands together. "Now that negotiations are done, send me in the direction of a ladder, and I'll work on the cameras while you ladies relax."

"I'll check the garage for one." Suz grabbed her crutches and swung down the front steps.

Nash moved in front of Ela. "My daughter, Lanie, has asked a lot of questions about the accident and Suz. Lanie wants you to know she prays for you and your sister every night."

"Thank her for remembering us."

"I wonder if you'd both join us for dinner on Sunday."

"Nash, I'm not dating, right now."

"It's just a meal."

She should have said no thanks and forgotten explanations. At least she hadn't gone into a long-winded story about her life with Aaron. How could she explain the myriad of emotions that attacked her when she spoke about him? She ran a hand through her hair, searching for the words.

He took her hand and faced her. "Are you hinting that if you have dinner with me I'll be the rebound guy, or that you feel guilty about dating, or that it's me?"

"Yes. Everything you just said, except it's not you." She was making a mess out of trying to make him understand why she'd turned down his invitation. And why was he holding her hand?

"Come quick," Suz hollered from the garage.

"It better not be a picture frame," Ela yelled, running down the steps with Nash at her heels.

CHAPTER 6

Nash and Ela raced through the open garage door.

Suz stood by the side window, her hand fisted. She opened her palm and stuck it under Ela's nose. "I found seven gum wrappers."

"You screamed about trash?" Ela folded her arms over her chest. "Seriously?"

"Where did you find the wrappers?" Nash studied the papers in Suz's hand, searching for a reason to yell.

"I found them on the floor by the window. They've gotta be from the scumbag who cut up mom's picture."

Nash took in the space. The concrete ground hid signs of footprints. The windowpanes on opposite sides of the building were locked, and the grimy sills appeared to have been untouched for ages.

"I'm not sure we should panic, Suz." Ela bit her lip and her gaze skittered around the space.

From her body language, Nash guessed she was trying to stay cool for Suz's sake, and Ela didn't want to say anything that would upset her sister further.

Suz leaned on a crutch and showed off the litter again. "Here's the proof someone hid in our garage and waited to break in."

"Did the police search the garage the other day?" Nash walked the floor's perimeter, considering the contents. Nothing struck him as out of place or unusual for a structure that stored garden tools, a lawnmower and bike.

"They did," Ela said, "but I'm sure gum wrappers weren't high on their clue list."

Nash crossed to the window behind Suz. "If you stand in this spot, you can look straight into your living room." His gut clenched.

"What?" The two women shouted and hustled forward to gaze into their house.

"We need blinds," Suz shrieked! Then backed away from the window. "He was watching us."

"So creepy." Ela shivered.

Nash stepped closer to the glass. "Given you found seven wrappers, I'd guess your trespasser stayed in this spot for a while."

"Major creepout. He spied on us for hours." Suz made a face as she balanced on her crutches.

Ela hugged her arms across her chest. "There must be a logical explanation. Either the police left the wrappers, or the wind blew them inside."

"Police buy Octopus Eight Gum?" Suz exhaled an annoyed breath. "I doubt *they'd* chew gum tied into the Octopus Eight Movie. And how could the wind carry them all to one spot by the window?"

"Could Tyler have left them? Is he a fan of Octopus Eight Gum?" Ela asked.

Nash focused on Suz. Was Tyler their trespasser? And if he was, would Suz admit it?

Suz shook her head. "Tyler does chew the gum, but he wouldn't go into an empty garage and stand around when he can sit in the parlor with us."

Of course, Suz considered Tyler above suspicion. "Did you lock the garage?" Nash asked.

"The doors don't have a lock," Ela said. "I should have installed deadbolts on every place with a hinge."

The wind theory was doubtful. He voted for the idea of a person bringing the gum with him. "Do you store valuables or antiques here?"

Ela waved a hand over the back wall. "No. I'm calling Chief Ballard."

"They better not accuse Tyler again." Suz stuck out her lower lip.

"Ballard accuses everyone." Nash stepped closer to the shelves. Nothing stood out as valuable.

"Detectives get paid to suspect people," Ela lectured. "I understand your bias, Suz, but Nash, what's going on between you and the Chief?"

"Lawyers get paid to look at all angles for the truth. Ballard feels that's his job, not mine. Store any combustibles?" Nash asked, turning away from her. Good thing their trespasser hadn't had arson on his mind.

"Nothing flammable." Ela shook her head. "Excuse me, while I use my phone." She turned on her heel and went outside.

Suz turned on her crutches toward Nash. "I always thought it'd be cool to be in a real life horror movie, but I've changed my mind."

"Come on, Suz," Nash said. "We'll go outside and watch for the police." He led her into the fresh air. "Remember, in those movies there's always a hero who rescues the women in trouble."

"You should tell that to Ela," Suz said with a hint of suggestion in her voice. "But she won't believe it. You're a lawyer, and she doesn't want anything to do with them. They gave my dad bad advice during his trial and took what was left of our money. Plus, she's not into dating. Did you always want to be a lawyer?"

"I resisted the call for years, but when my daughter Lanie was born I decided to go to law school and make a good life for my family. How about you? Do you hold a grudge against my occupation?"

"Well, not you, anyway. You ordered pizza. You can stick around for a while. Don't feel too bad. It's not just that you're a lawyer. Ela was engaged and is still dealing with her breakup."

"She told me."

"Ela told you about *Aaron*?"

"Is he a national secret?"

"She never talks about *him*."

The ending must have been painful, Nash thought. How much had she loved her ex, and what has she still not told him about Aaron Wright?

"I wish the police would find who chewed the gum."

"I hope they do, too. Let's move to the porch."

Once there, Suz hovered near a wicker chair. "If the police

arrest the creep who spied on us, you won't represent him, will you?"

"No, Suz, I won't."

"Chief Ballard is in the neighborhood," Ela announced as she swung open the screen door to join them. "He'll be here in a few seconds."

"Did you notice the cops are always around except the night of my accident?"

"Be happy we got a quick response." Ela sank onto the wicker seat.

At the sound of an engine approaching, Nash spotted Ballard's black SUV. "He gives new meaning to quick and suspicious."

Suz tracked the vehicle traveling toward them. "Ballard could be the one spying on us. If we were in a horror movie, he'd be the bad guy."

"Please, Suz," Ela held up a hand. "Don't make our lives worse by accusing the police chief. And Nash, is there something we should know about Chief Ballard?"

Nash kept a steady gaze on the chief, who always approached people with his intimidating scowl. "The man has accused too many of my clients for me to bond with him."

"Isn't it natural for a policeman to suspect someone who hires you?" Ela asked.

"He's irrational."

Suz plopped down on a wicker chair and balanced the crutches against the furniture's arm. "He's going to ask those boring questions again. Where were you? Who was with you last night? Blah, blah."

"Suz, enough." Ela shot her sister a cease and desist look.

"I'm just saying." Suz said.

Chief Ballard's vehicle turned into the driveway.

"He's here for us. Give him a chance," Ela said, and rose to greet the chief as he climbed out of his SUV. On his uniform, he wore the Town of Rockypoint Patch and a badge stamped with the seal of New Hampshire.

His blue eyes scanned the neighborhood as though clues lay out in the open for him to view. His shoes thudded as he came up the porch stairs. He paused to nod to the women and frown at Nash. "McCain. No ambulances to chase?"

"I'm good. How about you? No speed traps to set up?"

Ela stepped between the two men, "Now that the pleasantries are out of the way, and we're all feeling closer to each other—"

Ballard jerked his attention to Ela. "Miss Danforth, why do you need an attorney when I speak to you?"

"Miss Danforth and her sister are *friends* of mine." Nash moved to Ela's side.

The glower in Ballard's eyes reminded Nash of a bull contemplating destroying the bullfighter. In fact, if Nash were the wimpy type, he'd back away and give Ballard a five-foot range. Instead, he edged closer.

"Chief Ballard, please take a seat, and I'll explain the whole situation." Ela pointed to a wicker chair.

"I prefer to stand." He dug a hand into his pocket and produced his notepad. From behind his ear, he removed a pen. "You had another break-in." Ballard poised his pen over the pad. "What happened?"

Ela compressed the facts about the latest discovery into a three-minute summary for him. Suz glared at Ballard throughout the summation. No doubt, she was silently daring him to mention Tyler's name.

The chief pressed his lips together in a tight, thin line while he scribbled notes until Ela explained the wrappers. "You called me because you found gum wrappers?"

Suz sat upright in her seat, keeping her broken leg in front of her. "Someone was in our garage and looked into our window while he or she chewed Octopus Eight Gum. Right, Nash?"

Nash could hear a bee buzzing in the front yard as everyone waited for his confirmation or denial. "Absolutely."

Ballard grunted.

"Could one of the officers from the other night have dropped the wrappers?" Ela asked in a quiet voice.

"I'll have their tails if they did, but I check every possibility." The chief closed his notepad and stared at Suz. "I understand you hang out with Tyler Rawlings. He's trouble."

Suz raised her chin. "You shouldn't say bad things about him while an attorney is present." She smiled for the first time. "Did you hear him, Nash?"

"Unfortunately."

Ela repositioned herself next to Suz. "I'm sure Chief Ballard was trying to offer friendly advice."

Ballard tapped his pen against the notepad. "If a high school student raced up Moose Hill and forced your sister off Dead Man's Curve in a sick game, we'll bring charges against him or her."

Suz struggled to her feet.

Ela caught her arm. "Suz, sit and rest your leg while the Chief speaks."

Her sister sank back against her chair with a huff.

"Let's hear what he's dug up." Nash leaned his hip against the railing. He'd be surprised if Ballard offered them one new detail, but Ela needed help, or at least a lead.

"I don't give out the facts of an ongoing investigation. Look, McCain. I don't know who you're planning to sue today, but go bother them because I don't answer to you."

"Shouldn't you investigate the garage where the wrappers were found?" Ela said, motioning him toward the former carriage building and away from Nash, without results.

"Outside of these wrappers," Ballard said, "you've no other proof someone was spying on you?"

"We have my mother's headless picture," Suz interjected.

"Miss Danforth," Ballard continued. "Have you seen these wrappers before today? What about you?" The chief switched his gaze to Suz. "Do your friends buy this gum?"

"The gum's for sale at all the stores," Suz said, and jutted out her lower jaw.

Ballard's interrogation only made Suz clam up, Nash thought. She wasn't about to admit her boyfriend bought the gum.

Ela shook her head and added, "I've never seen a wrapper before today."

"And nothing is missing from your home?" Ballard asked.

"We haven't gone through the rooms yet," Ela admitted, biting her lip, "but we did the other night when the patrol came."

Was Ballard trying to make Ela feel foolish? Irritation dissolved Nash's handful of patience. "Miss Danforth's knowledge of gum wrappers is unimportant and doesn't change that a person spied on Ela and her sister."

"We're not in court, McCain." Ballard turned to Ela. "Your

neighborhood patrol is two blocks away. I'll call them. They'll check your house and garage while you stay outside. You do seem to have a lot of problems at your place."

"Ela and her sister have gone through enough without you hinting that they're trouble," Nash snapped.

"I'm stating a truth. My phone's in the car." Ballard marched to his vehicle.

"I wish he'd disappear," Suz whispered.

"I understand the feeling," Nash agreed.

"We don't have to be best friends," Ela said. "But he did come when I called."

"Hello, it's his job." Suz threw out her palms. "He'd like to arrest Tyler for my accident and probably the break in, too. Cops hate teenagers. They have teendar."

Nash watched the chief phone his men. "Ballard has his radar out for everyone, Suz." And especially me.

* * *

Less than an hour later, the police left, declaring they found no signs of a trespasser and muttering to each other about the bubblegum intruder. Nash helped Ela hang onyx-colored curtains from the attic over the parlor windows. Finally, they settled in the dining room where the odor of hot pizza filled the air and the overhead antique bronze lamp provided a soft glow. Suz sat, drumming her fingers on the tabletop. Her brows furrowed.

"Your pizza isn't getting any warmer," Ela said from her seat at the end of the dining room table. All she wanted was to get through the meal without more drama.

Nash leaned over the arm of his chair toward Suz. "We won't tell your boyfriend you ate the competitor's."

"His is the best. Ela, I think the person who spied on us is someone who hated us in New York because of Dad."

Ela wished her sister would refrain from talking about their problems in front of Nash. "Thanks, Suz, for pointing that out."

"Whoever it is, is a coward, hiding all the time." Suz tore off a piece of pizza and shoved it into her mouth.

"I noticed the new locks on the doors," Nash said. "Nice job installing them."

"Ela put them in the day I found the headless picture. Next time you visit, Nash, she'll have bars on the windows."

"I already bought baby blue ones to match your phone," Ela said in between bites.

Suz dropped her slice. "You didn't buy bars, did you?"

"Guess you'll find out."

"Funny, El. All I know is Tyler's innocent. I think it's definitely someone from New York. I don't think anyone hated Aunt Vickie. Even the squirrels loved her." Suz bit into her food.

Ela wriggled in her seat, unable to sit still while her sister aired their private life, and Nash sat less than an elbow length away. The idea of repaying him for all he was doing for her added to her squirm quotient. She shoved to her feet. "Nash, can I refill your lemonade?"

Suz raised her hand. "I'll take a glass of wine."

"Dream on, sister. Nash?"

"I'm set."

Ela sat again. In the silence, Nash stared at her for the next few seconds until he turned to her sister.

"Suz, your discovery of the gum wrappers warrants an A plus, but Ela is right. You can't dream up theories. We need proof." He paused. "Moving on to a new topic, I want to invite you both to dinner at my mother's house on Sunday. We usually gather there after church. I hope this date works for you, Ela. Are you lovely ladies free?"

Meet Nash's family? Prickles ran up Ela's arms. "I appreciate the invitation, but—"

"Can Tyler come?"

"Absolutely."

"Cool. Oh, no, he's working." Suz sipped her drink before spilling the next fact. "You don't have to worry about Ela. She's always free."

"Thanks, Suz, for the update on my calendar." Why had her parents wanted a second child? "I scheduled a meeting with a realtor about listing Aunt Vickie's store. I can't postpone."

"What time is your appointment?"

"Noon."

"We'll expect you—"

"Why don't you and your daughter come here?" Suz interjected. "We can eat the lasagna in the freezer after the appointment. Didn't my sister say she owed you a meal for putting in the cameras?"

Suz was up to something. "Nash and his daughter are expected at his mother's."

"We can work it out." He flashed a smile that suggested he'd be more than pleased to come. "I know my dad and mom have other guests and won't mind. Lanie and I often skip a week due to scheduling conflicts."

Ela searched her mind for another excuse. Dinner on Sunday with Nash McCain was too much like a date. Finding no other reason to turn him down, she jumped to her feet. She needed to rid herself of the anxiety she felt. "Let me clean up. Anyone want chocolate cake?"

Suz grimaced. "I couldn't eat one more calorie." She tossed her crust on to the plate.

After Nash refused another piece, Ela gathered the dirty plates with lightening speed and carried them into the kitchen. Suz followed behind on her crutches.

Ela set the dishes on the counter before she lowered her voice and spoke. "I don't know what you're planning, but I know it's not because you enjoy sharing lasagna that you invited Nash and his daughter."

"Okay, Tyler works all the time. It's always you and me alone in this empty house. Besides Tyler's mad at me and won't be here on Sunday. I don't want to sit around on the weekend, thinking about him."

"What happened?"

"He's bummed I don't want to marry him."

"Marry?" She must be suffering from a hearing loss.

"Yeah. He thought we should get married to make you happy about moving in together, after I told him I couldn't live with him because you'd go crazy, but I don't want to be a wife while I'm in high school. My diploma would have a Mrs. on it." She wrinkled her nose.

Ela stifled her impulse to lecture. Treading lightly would be the best strategy. "Suz, please consider the police believe Tyler might be guilty of a burglary in town, and not the best person to date."

"He's not a thief." Suz stamped her foot. "I have to believe him, Ela." Suz lowered her voice. "He's my boyfriend, and he's good to me even though we hit a few speed bumps."

"Maybe he's hiding his true self."

"Ela, just because someone is nice to you doesn't mean they'll turn around and treat you like dirt." Suz raised her chin, walked away and stopped to whirl around. "I have to give Tyler the benefit of the doubt. He's the only person who's been decent to me since everything happened with Dad."

"I worry he's taking advantage of you."

"I'm not dumb, El. I believe in him. *We* used to believe in people. What happened to you?" She didn't wait for an answer but left the kitchen.

"And look where it got us," Ela said to the empty room.

Nash's words about people helping others floated into her mind. She'd believed friends would lend a hand to help them when they ran out of money. Instead, they'd turned their backs and she'd lost her home, father, fiancé and job. She was done being trusting.

She crumpled a napkin and tossed it in the trash. On a scale of one to ten, how difficult was it to fool Suz? Probably a minus one.

From her pocket came the ring of her phone. She checked the cell phone window. It was *him*.

Okay, she'd answered before and all he'd done was spout worthless words at her. She wasn't afraid of *him*.

"Hello."

"The wicked are estranged from the womb: They go astray and are punished as—"

Her stomach cramped at the sound of his voice.

"Don't call me again or I'll be forced to report you." She clicked off her phone and tossed it on the counter. *I'm finished with him.*

But the nagging voice in the back of her mind whispered, "Never."

69

CHAPTER 7

Friday evening, Nash brought Lanie to her grandmother's for the night and promised to pick her up before the lasagna dinner on Sunday. They said their goodbyes, and he was halfway to the door when she ran after him. "Dad, Dad, did mom like lasagna?"

"Lasagna?" From the past sprang the scene of dirty dishes piled in the sink, and Cindy sitting in the kitchen chair still in her bathrobe. She held three-year-old Lanie on her lap, hungry and crying.

"Dad?"

His mind cleared, and he crouched down to her. "Your mom loved it."

Lanie smiled. "I thought she did. I do too. Bye." She whirled around and ran off to her grandfather.

Nash stood unmoving, struck by a new question. Why didn't he remember if Cindy ate pasta? He'd suppressed the painful memories of his wife to the point that the trivial facts had become lost.

Hopefully Lanie wouldn't ask more questions he couldn't answer. He headed to his office.

The streetlights snapped on as he parked at the curb. In his office, he pulled the shades and booted up his computer. The absence of the remodeling sounds was a blessing. With the night his own, he had plenty of time to search for information about Ela Danforth and her family.

He found one article from the local paper online. The headline announced the opening of her aunt's antique shop, Now and Then. He read it as well as several brief ads for the store's anniversary sales through the years. Finally, he found a piece that included a note about a brass bed, a wedding gift from Vickie to her sister, Lizzie. The item pointed him toward the marriage in New York and the groom Matt Blanchette.

Links about investment fraud, Matt Blanchette's arrest and sentencing to federal prison for fifty years filled the screen when Nash searched for Blanchette's name. After reading the paper, he understood how much Ela wanted to further herself from her father's criminal legacy and adopted their mother's maiden name as one strategy. Finished, Nash opened the email about Ela from his godfather, Uncle John.

The older man lived and breathed the happenings of the Big Apple, and Nash had written him for information on the trial. Nash scanned the letter. Family news from his uncle overflowed the first two paragraphs. At the end of the email, the older man answered Nash's questions.

"Local law enforcement and the feds took a hard look at Miss Danforth, but no charges were brought against her. Whatever Michaela Blanchette's money problems are, if they connect to her father, Matt Blanchette, you can't help her. I recommend a financial lawyer experienced in federal cases. Blanchette's arrest for fraud and a host of other crimes was a media circus here in the city."

Uncle John quoted a news article to provide a better understanding of the atmosphere surrounding the financier.

"'Victims of Matt Blanchette held daily rallies outside the courthouse during the trial. They cursed the defendant for their losses and sufferings. Many spit on the family members who dared showed their faces.'"

Nash clicked off the email and searched for a link containing further information. He found a site with a grainy picture of a small woman with curly, rust-colored hair. The caption read: Michaela Blanchette, daughter of the defendant, at the courthouse."

He enlarged the photo. Ela stood alone, beside a limo, staring at the crowd held back by a police line. Her mouth was tight, and her eyes were wide with fear or shock. Was she reacting to a crude remark or the mass of people? Why was she alone?

Her reaction when she accepted his hand at the hospital

floated into his mind, and he understood her hesitation better.

He fisted his hands and searched the faces in the throng. One of them could have followed her to Rockypoint out of revenge. Being robbed of your life savings served as a big motivator to leave your hometown.

He recalled the day he and Ela went to the hospital, and the SOC protestors had blocked the hospital's main entrance. If only he had a picture of the group to compare with the New York gathering. He hit print and sat back to stare at Ela's photo while the printer whirred to life. Where was her sister, mother or Aunt Vickie when she went to her father's indictment? At the thought of family, he picked up his phone. He needed to say good night to Lanie again and tell her he loved her.

The next afternoon, Nash left home early and arrived at the Danforth house. He parked in the drive, walked to the front porch, rang the doorbell and waved to the overhead camera. In minutes, the door swung open three inches to reveal Suz Danforth on her crutches in jeans and a chambray shirt. "Nash, you're early." She opened the door wider.

"Good afternoon, Suz. I stopped by to see if you needed anything for our meal."

She peered past him. "Isn't your daughter coming?"

"She's at her grandmother's, but her grandfather has offered to drop her off in half an hour. Don't worry. Lanie can't wait to come."

"Great." Suz flicked a glance over her shoulder and back.

"Am I interrupting?"

"Ela left an hour ago, and I thought I heard a strange noise. I'm sure it was nothing, but would you—"

"I'd love a tour of your home. Mind?" He put one foot on the threshold.

"Come in." She started to move aside and paused. "Don't tell Ela a noise freaked me, will ya? She'll never leave me alone again."

"Your secret will never pass my lips. Where'd the noise come from?"

"It came from one of the bedrooms upstairs." Suz closed the door and locked up while he strode toward the steps.

"Hold on." She moved in front of him, her face taut. "One

more thing. Don't mention I let you in her room. She's strange about people visiting her space."

"I'm a lawyer. Circumspect is my middle name."

"Nash Circumspect McCain. It sounds lawyerish." She hobbled up the stairs to the second floor and into the first room. "Behold the inner sanctum known as my sister's bedroom or Aunt Vickie's guest room."

He strode into a room wallpapered with lavender flowers. An off-white bedspread and a small dressing table decorated with matching fabric completed the decorations. The lilac fragrance Ela wore hung in the air. "Very feminine."

"Ela said the room's busy like Aunt Vickie." He crossed the rug and opened the closet to find rows of dark clothes. "No one's inside." He picked up the bed skirt for a quick glance underneath. "Nothing is there either, not even a dust ball."

"Ela would rather find a thief under her bed than dust. I'll show you the rest of the house."

In fifteen minutes, they'd gone through the remaining rooms and the garage. Suz tagged along beside him until they reached his car in the drive. He snatched keys from his pocket. "How about you answer a question?"

"I guess I owe you. What?"

"Why did you invite me to dinner?"

She shrugged and glanced around the yard before she leveled her gaze on him. "I invited you because you helped Ela."

"What else?"

She balanced on the crutches and dragged the toe of her shoe in front of her, drawing an imaginary line. "I've a deal for you. When Chief Ballard interrogated me, he asked if Tyler knocked me off the road. He believes Tyler is guilty of trying to hurt me. He's always warning me and Ela about him."

"Why would your boyfriend harm you?" A piece was missing from her story.

She raised one shoulder in a shrug. "He wouldn't. But we had a fight about moving in together outside school the day of my accident. Some big mouth reported it to a teacher who told the police."

"Does Ela know all of this?"

"Most of it. Tyler's not guilty and needs a lawyer. I looked

73

you up on the internet. You've done wicked cool cases, Nash. We want to hire you, but we can't afford your prices."

"By we, you mean—"

"Tyler and I discussed it. He agreed that you'd be awesome as his lawyer."

"What about Ela? Did she vote?"

"She doesn't know." Suz ducked her head and avoided eye-contact. "She'd feel obligated and discourage the whole thing."

"Tell her, and then I'll take Tyler on."

"You have to understand. Ela would die of thirst in the desert while someone held out a glass of water to her because taking the drink would mean she owed him."

"Sounds harsh and I suspect not true."

"Mostly true. I don't agree with her, but I don't expect charity either. I could sit for you. Do you have a regular sitter?"

"Grandparents fill in when I need one."

"I—" Suz jerked her thumb at herself "—can come anytime I'm not at school. I can stay over at odd hours, and in return, you represent Tyler. It's a win-win."

"Have you considered a future in the law?"

"Ela would disown me. I can give you references. I printed a list." She dug out a folded sheet of paper from her pocket. She held it up and gave him a rare smile that showed off the promise of a beautiful young woman.

He read through the names and addresses. All were residents in New York. "Thanks, Suz. Lanie could use a little girl time. Can you hit a ball or play hopscotch?"

"Are those the interview questions?" She wrinkled her nose. "I spent most of my free time as a kid practicing ballet, but I'm sure I can manage to hop in a square or hit a little ball once I'm off these crutches."

"Excellent. You can teach Lanie a few ballet steps, too." He extended his hand. "Tell Ela, and we've a deal."

* * *

From her store, Ela watched as the gray car parked at the curb, and the baby-faced real estate agent, Kevin Johnson, hopped out. He patted down his neat brown hair and sprinted toward the shop. He bolted through her door and drew to a halt in front of her on the other side of the glass counter case.

"It's good to see you again, Miss Danforth. Sorry, I'm late." He gripped her hand for a firm handshake. "I was at a closing, and the buyer's agent insisted on inserting an unexpected clause. We spent an extra ten minutes hammering it out."

"You brought good news, I hope." She gestured to the portfolio under his arm.

"I've researched stores and buildings in this section of town and prepared the comps for you." He shoved aside a pile of knickknacks to set his file on the glass surface with a plop. He pulled out a folder of papers and launched into a detailed report on the age, location and recent sale price of each pictured piece of real estate.

After three minutes of his spiel, Ela laid her hand on top of the next sheet before he could continue his sales pitch.

His jaw dropped open. "What's wrong?"

"Give me the bottom line, the price. What can you sell Now and Then for?"

"Based on the most recent sale comps, I'm confident I can get the top value for your property." He whipped out a paper from the bottom of the stack and held it out to her.

The number burst the bubble of hope in her chest. She'd sell the place and still be in debt. "This seems low."

"If you study the comps—"

She waved a hand at him. Aunt Vickie owed two months' rent on three storage units, and the quarterly property taxes were due, along with the monthly utilities. Ela rubbed her forehead. She needed to get a grip. Some money was better than none. "What's the average number of days on the market at this listing price?"

He pointed at the sheet of statistics. "Most retail stores in Rockypoint sell in an average of a year with the exception of Cupid's Cupcakes, which went within a week."

Now he was talking. "How did they sell so fast?"

"She sold the business to her mother."

Ela's optimism died. "That won't work for me. There must be another option? Do you do auctions?"

"If you read my final page, you'll find the most recent public sale was for Pete's Convenience Store." He leafed through the sheets. "I don't usually recommend auctions because they draw people looking for a steal."

She leaned over the counter as he found the paper with the convenience store blueprints and laid it in front of her. "Pete's sold for thirty-seven thousand."

"Thirty-seven is a pittance. How large was it?" She peered at the storefront's footage on the prints. Which rectangle on the paper was Pete's?

"The price included the entire plaza."

"What?" She snapped upright. "You can't be serious. Why would he sell for such a low amount?"

"Buyers do their homework. They smell desperation and bid low. The owner accepted the offer to pay the bank. Lots of sharks attend auctions."

"Great. I'll bring spear guns to mine."

"If we price too high, the building will stay on the market for sure."

"I'll think about it and let you know. I appreciate your meeting with me today." She shook his hand to end the conversation.

"You can call my cell." He scooped up the documents and stuffed them in his organizer. "I'll be expecting to hear from you."

Too bad a few hours or days wouldn't make a difference in the store's value or her answer. She didn't have much choice. At least the hospital allowed her to pay a small amount each month toward Suz's bill. Ela walked the realtor to the door.

"You can use the quiet to think on it." He glanced down the empty street. "Funny, to think this used to be the center of downtown before the big chains built on the other end and drew the shoppers away."

Ela moved onto the sidewalk and followed his gaze down the block. On the corner sat the tattoo parlor that was closed on Sundays. Across the street stood the bar Momma Won't Find Out. Scattered over the rest of the street were two thrift shops, a used furniture store and several boarded-up storefronts. For Rent signs decorated their display windows and weeds sprouted in the cracks of the sidewalks.

The facades did not say, "Buy me."

"This section was once booming," Kevin said. "Times are tough in Rockypoint, Miss Danforth. The manufacturing plant's closing was the final blow. A lot of people lost their jobs and incomes. The big box chains survived because corporate funneled money from their more successful stores outside our area to keep the local ones alive."

She swept a gaze over the brick front. Thank goodness her aunt wasn't around to witness the sale of her shop. Sadness crept over Ela.

"I'll get what I can for your business," he said, interrupting her thoughts. "As far as most people are concerned, it's just another used furniture store like the one on the next street."

"Thanks for the pep talk." The man was sure a downer.

"Wish I had better news. Have a good afternoon." He crossed the sidewalk to his vehicle.

The sun dipped behind a cloud as the real estate agent's car shot away. A chill hung in the air. Ela closed the door and on impulse, turned the lock. She replayed the realtor's forebodings in her head. She'd overestimated the profit from the store's sale. Now she'd have to stretch her paycheck a little further. She tried to view the antique shop with a buyer's eye. The inside of Now and Then didn't welcome customers. The furniture stood in piles. Mounds of knick-knacks covered the counters. Aunt Vickie must have been too ill to take care of her new arrivals.

If Ela wanted to sell, she'd have to be sure the place grabbed a buyer's attention. On the other hand, if she held an estate sale first, the person in charge took care of the set-up.

The sound of something scurrying overhead sent a ripple of goose bumps over her skin. Rats? That settled it. She was finished for today. From behind the counter, she grabbed her purse and coat. She double checked her pocket for the pepper spray and locked up. Nash was arriving at her house in twenty minutes. She'd barely arrive home before he showed up. Why had she agreed to this meal? Why hadn't she protested more and explained she needed to work?

At least Tyler wasn't joining them. On the street, a navy sedan eased to a stop at the green light. Strange. She slowed. Once she crossed the street, she would be in the worst section of town.

She turned toward the used bookstore and pretended to browse the window of the closed shop. Out of the corner of her eye, she watched the indigo-colored car turn left and away from her. Now, she'd hotfoot it. She crossed into the next block at a trot. The sound of an engine alerted her to a vehicle behind her. She glanced back.

The sedan that had stopped at the intersection was cruising toward her. It must have turned around. Wasn't this the same vehicle that had been on her street when Nash showed up at her house? Of course, in a small town, it wasn't that unusual to see a similar car again and again.

To be safe, she broke into a jog. A twenty-four hour convenience store loomed ahead. She'd get his license plate number and then duck inside the mart. Timing would be everything.

"Ela! Ela!"

She whirled around and spotted Nash's sports car coming toward her. He leaned out of the window and waved to her.

She ran toward him, pausing at the curb where he stopped.

Down the street, the sedan took a left turn and disappeared. She jumped inside Nash's two-seater and locked her seatbelt into place, taking reassurance from the simple click.

"Wow, you could make leaping into an auto an Olympic sport. You'd earn the gold."

"I'm excited about that lasagna."

"I was hoping you were happy to see me."

"I am. What are you doing in this neighborhood?" She ran a hand through her hair and then smoothed the collar of her fleece jacket to give herself time to think. Was she imagining trouble because she was upset over the sale of Now and Then? No matter, she wasn't about to whine about her problems to Nash.

"Your sister said you were walking home from the store. Since Lanie's getting a ride from her grandfather, I was free and thought you'd like a lift."

"I appreciate it." She shoved her hair out of her face and peered at the side mirror and then through the rear window. The shadowing car was not in sight.

"Everything okay?" He shifted into drive. "You keep looking out the window."

"I noticed a Cadillac type of car stopped at the green light. Isn't that odd?"

"Maybe the driver was finishing up a call or figuring out directions. Did it cause a traffic jam? Where is it?"

"We've no traffic to jam, and it's gone now." His explanation made sense. She'd better not confess that imaginary stalkers or rats in the attic scared her.

"Is someone following you?"

"If they are, they're doing a terrible job by driving in the wrong direction. Besides, I told you I'm paranoid." He was frowning. "Don't worry, we don't need Ballard." But if he drove faster, she'd be at home, away from unreal threats.

"If you see the vehicle again, call me and Ballard right away."

"Will do. Are you driving slow?" She gestured at the speedometer, wishing they'd whisk past the area.

"We're in a thirty miles per hour zone. I was hoping to get a tour of your store to report to my mother. Her motto when she shops is: if it's old, it's sold."

"And she never met my Aunt Vickie? I thought everyone knew everyone."

"I've never asked her." He gave her his winning grin. "I'm flattered you remember what I told you about Rockypoint."

Just like a man. She peered into the side mirror once more. No sedans in view. At least she could relax. "Why did you talk to Suz?"

"I wondered if you needed anything for dinner and stopped at your place a few minutes ago. Suz had everything under control. You must really miss your car. I expected to twist your arm to convince you to take a ride. I know you weren't too happy your sister invited us."

"I'm sorry about my attitude the other day." Ela massaged the small ache in her forehead. "I do miss Aunt Vickie's antique vehicle." She slid a gaze toward his profile.

He reached over and squeezed her hand in a reassuring manner. "Sure you're okay?"

"Fine." Today should be about thanking him, not burdening him with personal problems. Besides, she could handle it. "The thought of Suz slaving away reheating food in the kitchen is a shocker. I'm surprised you trusted us enough to bring your daughter."

"Why not? I'll be there."

"Did you spot a sign of Tyler?"

"No. Do you have a lot of family dinners?"

"We don't have relatives nearby." His questions left her uneasy. "How about you? Do you have lots of aunts and uncles who love to come to share your food and ask personal questions?"

"I'm an only child, but a lot of my cousins settled nearby. We're never lonely."

He rode through an area that consisted of apartment buildings and single homes. She kept track of the traffic ahead and behind, in case the sedan returned.

"I'm sorry to bring this up, but you seem preoccupied."

"Sorry, finding the gum wrappers in our garage unnerved me."

"You can unwind today. Nothing big will happen unless Suz burns the dinner."

"Don't temp fate."

"Since we're talking family, what about your former fiancé?"

Ela folded her hands in her lap and squeezed them together. Her house was coming up.

She'd get the discussion of Aaron over quickly. "What do you want to know?" she asked as he turned onto her street.

"I have a feeling there's more to his story."

She didn't have to tell Nash everything about her ex. Keep it short and to the point, and the doubts and pain will stay under control.

"Aaron drowned. He's gone. Forever. What else do you want to know?"

CHAPTER 8

"I'll give you some background if that's what you'd like." She'd compress the information before they reached her house. "The pressures from my father's trial were tremendous, and the new DA wanted to make a name for himself. He dug deeper into my life and Aaron's. Both Aaron and I heard rumors from reliable sources that he'd be arrested after the weekend. Aaron wanted to get away from everyone and do what he loved, head out on his boat into the ocean to fish." She paused, clutching her purse to her chest before continuing. "He left Friday afternoon and never came back. His boat was located, but he wasn't on it."

"You must have been devastated, Ela."

At least Nash understood. "Everybody was. His father refused to believe he was gone and spent tons of money searching. The DA was suspicious, and he questioned Aaron's friends and relatives, but no one had seen him after he took his boat out on the ocean."

"I know firsthand how difficult losing someone can be," he said in a low voice.

"There's a little more," she said, debating how much she wanted to tell him. "My father offered Aaron a position as our firm's lawyer when we became engaged. My dad had hired him on a per diem basis until we announced we were tying the knot. If it weren't for me, Aaron wouldn't have become involved in our business at that level and fallen under investigation."

"Sounds like you blame yourself and think the investigators wouldn't have pulled him in for questioning if he had worked part time."

"It's not that simple."

"No, it's not. When my wife, Cindy, died, I held the world record for prayers asking why and what I could have done to save her. Over the months, I discovered I had to forgive myself and then the rest of the answers came."

Her chest tightened with each of his words. She couldn't go on with this discussion.

"I employ an investigator who can find anyone. If you think there's a chance your fiancé is on an island or in a country without extradition, I can contact my investigator about Aaron."

She shook her head. "Enough money has been wasted. Unless your P.I. is free, don't bother. There's no point in wasting money and stirring up expectations without results. The most we could hope would be for Aaron's body to be found washed up on a beach, and then we'd give him a decent burial."

"Understood."

"We're almost home. Please, don't bring up Aaron's death to Suz. I can't predict if she'll cry or act like she could care less. Worse, it brings up my father. She's not able to accept that he won't be around."

"I understand." The sun shone down on the silver SUV parked at the curb in front of her house. "My dad beat us here." They pulled into the drive, and Lanie jumped out and ran to her father's sports car as he cut the engine.

"Where's your grandmother?" Nash asked, getting out of the driver's side to greet her.

"She's resting. She's tired from playing Parcheesi all day."

"It's only noon, Lanie."

"Grandma said it felt like we played all day. I won five times. I told her thank you before I left." Lanie focused on Ela, who had joined Nash. "Hello, Miss Danforth. Thanks for inviting me to dinner."

"You're welcome, and please call me Ela."

"May I, Dad?"

"She gave you permission."

Dressed in khakis and a blue, short-sleeved shirt, Nash's white-haired father strode toward them. "Hello, Miss Danforth, I'm Simon McCain."

Ela shook his hand and extended an invitation to join them.

"Sorry, I should get home to my wife. We're expecting old

friends to come by. I'm sure we'll have plenty of opportunities to get together soon. Enjoy your afternoon with Nash and Lanie." Simon strolled to his vehicle.

What had he meant by plenty of get-togethers?

Lanie chatted nonstop while they strolled up the steps and across the porch. Smoke greeted them in the entry hall.

Was her sister really burning down the house? "Suz! Suz!" Ela ran into the parlor where the smoke clouded the room. Coughing, she yelled for her sister again.

"Ela?" Suz swept in on her crutches. "What's wrong?"

"Something's on fire." Ela's eyes smarted.

Suz sniffed at the odor of burnt food. "Not anymore. We're good."

"What happened?" Ela tore back the curtains, opened the side windows and fanned the fresh air with her hand. Nash and Lanie worked on opening the other windows.

"I forgot to take the rolls out," Suz said. "The lasagna will be done in a few minutes, and I made a big salad." She directed a smile at Lanie, who stepped closer to the fresh air streaming inside.

"Hi, I'm Suz Danforth."

"I'm Lanie McCain. I love salad."

"Good. You can set the table. Follow me."

"All right. Can you walk fast on your crutches?" Lanie asked, following Suz into the kitchen. "I know a boy who won a race on them. He beat everyone in the second grade on Field Day."

What was going on with her sister? She was acting like the hostess with the mostest.

"Lanie and Suz are getting along better than sisters," Nash said, watching them disappear.

"Suz has her good points. The last few years have been tough on her." Ela relaxed her shoulders now that the mini crisis was averted. "Suz never made a salad in her life. You might want to skip it."

"I'll risk it."

"Consider that she burned the store bought rolls you pop into the oven for a few minutes?"

"I'm sure everything will taste wonderful, and we already know all the guests."

The doorbell rang.

"Hold your next thought." Ela crossed the rug and glanced up at the small screen attached to the outside camera. A skinny male wearing a red, white and blue uniform stood on their porch. He held a rectangular box, raised his head, and smiled at the camera.

Tyler. Ela flung the door open. "We're not eating pizza today. You must have the order mixed up."

"Suz called and told me she burnt the rolls. I brought over breadsticks. Super Tyler to the rescue." He laughed and then sobered. "Where is she?"

"She's busy in the kitchen. I'll give her the delivery." Ela reached for the box.

Tyler raised the bread above her head. "No can do. This food goes direct to the customer."

"We have guests for dinner," Ela said as Tyler pushed past her.

"I've enough for everyone." He sauntered into the parlor and paused by Nash hovering near the mantle.

"You're McCain." He held out his hand. "I'm Tyler from The Pizza Man Can."

"Ah, yes. I recognize the uniform and your name pin on it. What brings you round, Tyler from The Pizza Man Can?"

"Suz called him for bread," Ela announced, joining them. The dinner was not off to a good start.

"Best pizza in town. The Pizza Man Can does any combo you want. Give us a try." Tyler dug into his pocket. "Here's a coupon." He handed the paper slip to Nash. "We've a special until the end of the month: two large cheeses for the price of one." He disappeared into the dining area.

Ela swore her curls kinked with stress.

"If he bothers you, I can escort him out." Nash said with a smile.

"You're a bouncer, too?"

"You doubt my manhood, Miss Danforth? I wasn't in the military for nothing."

"I'm hoping Tyler leaves on his own after he delivers the bread. I should make sure he does." She started toward the kitchen.

"Let me." He grabbed her hand.

His touch surprised her, and she froze. For several seconds or minutes, they stared at each other. His hazel eyes with flecks of green widened with awareness as her pulse fast-forwarded with the horrible knowledge that she couldn't remain indifferent to him.

"Excuse…me," she muttered and moved to a safe distance—a buddy distance. The attraction was only natural. The man had offered support and good humor during a stressful period in her life. He'd be easy to get used to having around. As a friend.

"I'll go." He hooked his thumb over his shoulder. "I have an impressionable nine-year-old going on fifty in the kitchen." He hustled away as though he couldn't wait to get out of the room.

Maybe he felt the opposite of attraction when he touched her. She stood still, unsure what to do next. Her hand still tingled from their contact. Why couldn't she be attracted to the mailman or even Police Chief Ballard?

She should find out what was happening in the other room. Ela started for the kitchen when the doorbell chimed again. She did a u-turn and checked the camera. As if her thoughts had called him, Chief Ballard's uniformed body barred the front entrance. She crossed the room and entered the hall. "Chief, good to see you. Did you bring news?"

He stepped into the entry when she held the door wider. "I wanted to set your mind at ease. Your sister's blood work came back from the night of her accident. You don't have to worry about DUI charges."

"El, where do we keep the parmesan cheese?" Suz swung into the hallway on her crutches, followed by Tyler. "Chief Ballard, my sister didn't tell me she invited you too."

"The chief came by to inform us no charges will be brought against you for the accident." Ela gripped her hands together. Great. Tyler and Ballard together. Who'd drop by next, the SWAT team?

"Didn't mean to interrupt your party." The chief's gaze shifted to Tyler, and Ballard slid into legs-apart-arms-braced-hands-ready police stance.

"Why would they charge me?" Suz asked with a pout. "I was always the victim."

"Just procedure, Suz," Ela said to head off an argument.

"My dad found the cheese." Lanie ran into the hallway and

stopped short at the sight of the frowning chief. "Did something bad happen?"

"It's okay, Lanie. The adults are catching up." Ela smiled to reassure the girl, instead of her true thought. Nothing would be okay until the meal was over and everyone left.

"What's going on?" Nash asked, joining them.

Lanie gestured to Ballard. "I think he needs you, Dad."

"Ballard," Nash acknowledged.

"I'm here to speak to Miss Danforth."

"Everyone continue whatever you were doing." Ela forced a smile. "I'm speaking to the chief."

"I know what you think about my boyfriend." Suz looped her arm through Tyler's. "You were hoping to arrest someone, Chief Ballard. If you take Tyler, I go too."

"Suz, don't be ridiculous." Ela said with one hand clutching the doorknob.

"Your sister's right. He'd have brought the uniforms if he was going to arrest me," Tyler said. "He wouldn't take me by himself."

"What do you want, Ballard?" Nash demanded.

"He told me the blood work cleared Suz of DUI." Ela let out an exasperated sigh.

"I'd never drink and drive." Suz rolled her eyes.

"Cool," Tyler said. "Let's eat bread."

"I don't need you butting in, McCain." Ballard scowled at Nash.

A phone's ringtone played out in the hallway. Tyler slid his hand into his pocket and checked his phone. "It's work. I gotta go. Lots of people count on pizza for their lunch. Delivering is high pressure. People don't realize how hard it is."

Suz leaned over and kissed him. "Come by later?"

"I'm sure he's too busy saving the world from hunger." Ela put a hand near her eye where she felt a throb of pain, and ignored Suz's snarky glance.

"I'll be back," Tyler announced over his shoulder and bounded out of the house.

"I'm going, too," Ballard told her. "You need anything, you got my number."

Ela followed him onto the porch. "You're convinced it was

an accident on the hill?" She just needed to hear it one more time, to reassure herself all was well.

"If we find the driver of the other vehicle, I'll arrest him or her for reckless driving, but at this moment, we don't have evidence leading to anyone."

"Thank you, Chief."

He didn't bother to answer. He marched toward his car, and Ela withdrew inside.

"Now we can relax," Nash said, his worried gaze on her.

Lanie rushed to the door and shouted out, "Bye, Uncle Josh."

Uncle? Had she heard correctly?

Ballard raised a hand in the air and then turned to Lanie standing in the open doorway. "Are you coming to my games? My team's a winner this year."

Lanie shook her head, and Ballard walked on. She whirled around and ran into the kitchen to join Suz. What was going on? Ela locked up and returned to the parlor.

Nash was studying the new picture of her mother and aunt that Lanie had added to the mantle. "You've a strong resemblance to your aunt."

"Never mind *my* relatives." Ela folded her arms over her chest. "You have a close one in the driveway. What's the deal between you and Chief Ballard?"

"He never got over the fact I broke his homerun record in high school."

"What else, McCain? Give."

"He's my late wife's brother. He blames me for not taking care of his sister and has no use for me. *I'm* his dark secret. He doesn't like anyone to know we're related."

"I take it he wasn't the best man at your wedding. What about Lanie? Does he do the uncle thing with her?"

Nash shook his head. "Maybe if she looked more like her mother than a McCain he'd have a harder time blowing her off. Ballard holds me responsible for his sister's death. Cindy died of a drug overdose of her prescription medication."

"Nash, I'm so sorry. Don't talk any more about it." Wow. Invite a guest to dinner and bring up his wife's death. Way to go, Ela.

"There's not much else to say. You can fill in the dots.

Depression, meds…" His voice faded away.

Lanie reappeared and ran up to him. "I chopped up a carrot. I'm going to tell Grandma I used a vegetable knife."

"Let's save that surprise for Christmas." He slid his arm around his daughter's shoulders. "Or your twentieth birthday."

"Oh, Dad, you're funny."

"Dinner's ready," Suz yelled from the kitchen.

"Later, we should talk." Ela threw a look at him over his daughter's head before she walked to the kitchen with her guests. Her mind swam with the news. The police chief and Nash were related. Rockypoint *was* a small place.

* * *

He was so close, but not close enough. He needed a better plan. Keeping watch on the house and her comings and goings wasn't working. He expected his phone to ring and Money Bags to yell at him again. Did he think screaming at him would get the job done?

Money was just like his own old man. He used to rant and call him names all the time. That never worked. Ask the old man now. He'd got what was coming to him.

Little Miss Perfect would get hers, too. He'd show Money Bags. He'd show everyone. The end would be big and loud. He'd hit the front page of the paper again.

Then he'd be rich. Plenty of women would go out with him once he had the cash to spend. He'd go someplace warm, sit on the beach, drink and pick up hot bodies. His mouth watered. He'd go clean his gun and practice. Worse came to worst, he'd just shoot her and end it. He'd buy a better rifle if he decided to do that. He dug in his jean pocket and pulled out a stick of Octopus gum.

* * *

Monday evening, darkness swallowed up the rainclouds as Ela reached her block. She'd worked the evening shift at the library, and her stomach growled in anticipation of a late meal. As she walked, the memory of being followed by the sedan ran through her thoughts. Nash had appeared at the perfect moment. But she should have coped on her own. Cold raindrops fell on her head. The night the coastguard had informed her Aaron was missing had resembled this one—dark and rainy. Shaken, she'd called the Judge. His strong voice outlined his rescue plan had pumped her up with hope.

She'd ended the call, and a few minutes later, Aaron's brother Ray had phoned. "Have faith, he'll be found. I'm organizing a search separate from the coastguard's and my father's. Between the Judge and me, we'll bring him home for dinner."

The splatter of cool water hit near her feet as a truck sped past. She bent her head under the downpour and turned her thoughts to home, safety and dry clothes. Drenched, she reached her house and hurried across the sidewalk and up the porch steps.

In the hallway, she removed her dripping trench coat. "I'm home, Suz."

The grandfather clock's chimes answered.

She hung up her coat. "Suz?" Ela wandered into the parlor and snapped on the light. She stood still, listening for sounds of activity. "Anyone home?" Her sister always hung out in this room.

Ela hustled toward the kitchen, clenching her hands at her sides. The odor of pizza mixed with cigarette smoke drifted under her nose. Tyler had been here. She turned on the light. A piece of paper sat propped against the salt and pepper shakers on the table.

"Gone out. Be home soon. S."

At least she'd left a note. Ela's stomach growled in hunger. She changed into jeans and a jersey and had set to work making a sandwich when she caught sight of the empty pizza box on top of the counter. Reminders of Tyler were always around, but she had other things to do besides worry about his constant presence. With food in hand, she was ready to work on her furniture inventory. She'd finish up and get estimates for the estate sale, her one opportunity to get solvent.

She climbed to the second floor and began writing the name and condition of each piece of furniture. After completing the listing for two of the four bedrooms and eating her sandwich, she was on a roll. She stretched her back and checked her watch. More than an hour had passed since she'd arrived home, and Suz still hadn't returned. Obviously her sister's interpretation of 'soon' was different from Ela's.

She might as well go up to the third floor attic to keep busy. Ela seized her phone from her pocket. No missed messages. The sound of the rain pounding on the roof grew as she wound up the narrow staircase. The phone buzzed in her hand. Suz? She checked the caller ID.

He was calling. Her threat must have meant nothing to him. She hesitated and hit end. A new number would solve the problem. She stuffed the phone in her pocket. Under her feet, the stairs protested with loud creaks. She opened the door. Trapped chilly air surrounded her. She snapped on the overhead light and blinked into the shadows created by the yellow bulb dangling from the rafter. The pelting rain on the roof drowned out the household noises. Around her sat a mismatched collection of furniture and mirrors.

Ela settled on a footstool and rested the notebook on her lap. She flipped to the last page and wrote Attic on the top line. Her phone rang.

She checked the ID. Caller unknown. For sure, she wasn't answering that one either. She clicked it off and pressed Suz's number. Her sister's voicemail answered.

"Call me," Ela said and hung up. She set the phone beside her and started on a trunk of odds and ends. She placed the assortment of out of date calendars, pictures and magazines at her feet. What had Aunt Vickie found exciting about these dust collectors?

The ring of her doorbell broke her concentration. She froze. In the last month, they'd had fewer than six visitors, not counting the police. She tightened the grip on her pen. It could be Nash. They hadn't had a minute to talk in private yesterday, and she'd plenty to ask him. She laid her cell on top of her notes and jogged down the stairs.

When she reached the second floor, her cell phone rang. Shoot, she'd left it in the attic. It might be Suz. The buzzing of the doorbell continued followed by loud knocking.

"Just a minute," she yelled, and raced upstairs.

The phone's ringing stopped when she reached the third level. The caller's number was blocked and no message appeared. She blew out a breath of frustration and wound her way downstairs. The hall was silent when she landed on the first floor. She dodged into the parlor for a glance at the camera screen. No one was there.

She edged to the door. "Hello?"

No one responded. She threw on the outside light and then peeked out the front window. A shadowy form stood facing her. Then the shadow ducked behind the tree.

What? She spun away from the pane of glass. Her heart pounded in her ears. Was someone really out there, watching, trying to lure her to the door? She rubbed her eyes. Maybe it was just the tree's shadow and her overactive imagination.

She crept forward and angled to the side of the glass, scanning the yard. No signs of an unwelcome prowler, but closer to the driveway sat a refrigerator size box. She squinted at the box. An arm poked out of the opening. Blonde hair spilled over the side of the carton. Suz? No!

The floor seemed to dip beneath her feet. She couldn't catch her breath. She staggered to the house phone and pushed nine-one-one.

Please-oh-please, she must be wrong. It wasn't Suz out there. Not Suz.

A voice spoke to her from the receiver.

"I think someone hurt my sister. She's on the lawn in the rain and not moving."

The nine-one-one operator assured her a cruiser was in the vicinity, and if she needed the ambulance it would arrive in a few minutes.

Ela dropped the phone onto the floor, stepped over the receiver and peered outside. The rain hammered the cardboard. The middle sagged. Was her sister inside?

Ela unlocked the door and ran across the lawn. The heavy shower drenched her. Chills ran up and down her body. "Suz!"

She stopped a foot away. On the ground, the heavy rain darkened the blonde hair and beat it into the grass. The hand lay open and extended toward her. "S...uz?"

A black and white squad car pulled into her driveway.

No, please, no. Ela couldn't stop shaking as she pressed closer to the box.

"Hey, stop," the patrolman yelled, climbing out of his cruiser. She had to know. Ela dashed forward.

CHAPTER 9

A naked body spilled out of the box and onto the soaked ground. Ela wiped the rain off her face and blinked at the figure.

"Ma'am, move away." The patrolman, wearing a department issued raincoat, gripped her arm.

"It's...not my sister?" She looked into the charcoal eyes of the twenty-something-year old officer. Dark hair peeked out from under his uniform hat.

"I'm Officer Franklin, Ma'am. This is my partner, Officer Greene. You've a store mannequin on your front yard. Is this why you called?"

Ela straightened and her shoulders slumped with relief. "I thought it was my sister." Nerves in her stomach bounced up and down. "I thought I saw someone by the tree."

The officer's phone rang. "Nine-one-one is calling." He hit a button. "Officer Franklin. No, we don't need the ambulance. Okay." He tucked his phone in his pocket.

"Ma'am, move to the porch where it's dry. I'll look around the tree." Officer Franklin gestured toward the house.

She was already drenched.

The other officer stood near her. He was a chunky, older man and the lines in his face deepened as he spoke in a no-nonsense voice. "This way."

He escorted her up the steps to the porch. She remained by the railing while Officer Franklin beamed his flashlight by the tree and over the yard where the outdoor light didn't reach.

The older officer shifted in front of her and opened up his notebook. His small eyes bore into her as he rubbed the side of his long face. "Did you see who dumped the big doll in your yard?"

She shook her head. "Someone rang my doorbell. I went to answer, but no one was on the porch. I looked out the window and thought someone hid behind the tree and my sister was hurt and lying on the ground." Ela motioned toward the patrolman on the lawn, who snapped pictures of the dummy and measured the distance to the street.

The officer in front of her continued to ask basic questions. "Where was she when the doorbell rang? How long did it ring? Estimate the time it took to answer the door."

She talked, and he wrote until she asked, "Who'd do this?"

"It's probably a prank." He shut his notes. "You mentioned checking a camera."

"I've two video cameras, one over the back door and one over the front. I looked before I answered. No one was on the porch. They must have heard me on the stairs and ran to the edge of the lawn to watch."

A green sports car shot down the street. The brakes screeched. The vehicle turned into her drive and jerked to a halt. Nash had arrived.

"That guy's looking for a ticket," Officer Greene stated.

"Good luck. He's a lawyer," Ela said as relief rose up in her chest.

Nash jumped out and ignored the shout from the patrolman on the lawn. He raced up to Ela. "What happened? Are you okay?"

"Excuse me, sir." The older officer moved between Nash and Ela.

"The young lady's my client." Nash extended his hand. "I'm Nashua McCain." He seized the frowning officer's hand and pumped it. "Give us a minute to talk, and then I'll get out of your way."

"Miss Danforth is not under arrest. She was answering my questions," The patrolman snapped.

"Greene, come here," the other officer yelled across the lawn.

"We'll finish in a minute," Greene told her. He threw Nash a frown and thudded down the steps.

"Are you hurt?" Nash touched her shoulder in a show of concern.

"I'm fine." She nodded toward the mannequin. "Someone left me a gift. I thought it was Suz and I might have seen someone staring at the house. I'm not sure. It was dark and raining."

He tossed a glance at the mannequin and then stepped forward and put his arms around her. For a second, she stiffened. No more men in her life, whispered the promise in her head.

She absorbed the dampness of his leather jacket, the heat of his body, and the comfort he offered. She surrendered, resting her cheek against his broad chest and closed her eyes. It was heaven to have someone hold her, support her. The steady beat of his heart sounded in her ears. The scent of his pine soap mixed with the damp air.

He ran a hand over her hair. "I ran a red light on the way."

"You'd have to plead guilty." She swallowed the small wave of pleasure and broke free of his embrace. "How did you know what was happening at my house?"

"It's the old bad-news-travels-fast system."

His gaze seemed to devour her face.

"Your neighbor across the street knows my mother from church. She also noted my car in your drive a few times and put together we were friends. When the police arrived, she phoned Mom, hoping to get the scoop via me. You can guess the rest."

"She must have seen who left the box."

"I'm afraid not. She told my mother she'd just arrived home when the squad car pulled into your yard."

"We're her reality television. I'm grateful she called your mother." Ela inched closer to him, wanting his comforting warmth again.

"It's my turn to speak to the lady." Officer Greene's voice boomed across the yard as he trudged toward them. He stopped before her. "About the surveillance video."

Nash clapped his hands together. "I suggest we examine the tape. The machine is in the parlor cabinet where I set it up the other day."

"Hey, we're going to review the security recording," Officer Greene yelled to his partner.

Within minutes, Nash was playing it. Ela was too wound up to sit. Greene joined them to stand in front of the TV while Franklin stayed with the evidence outside.

At last she'd find out who was haunting her, and possibly, who'd hurt Suz on Dead Man's Curve.

A grainy video appeared with drops of rain dotting the lens. The poor quality ended her hopes. "We won't see anything." She clenched her hands at her sides.

"There!" Nash yelled. A shadowy form appeared on the front steps. A dark hoodie pulled over his head hid a face tilted downward.

Look up. Look up, Ela ordered him.

"He's spotted the camera," Nash said.

"Can you identify him?" the patrolman asked.

Nash moved closer. "His mother couldn't ID him."

Ela summoned up faces from her life in New York. First to float into her mind was the man in the walker. He'd sworn at her because he couldn't afford medication for his elderly wife after Ela and her father had stolen their money. Then there was the woman in her sixties who'd told Ela she'd had to beg for public assistance like a pauper. More and more of their voices poured into her head. All were angry and sad.

"He's no one I remember." She crowded closer to the screen, away from the others to swipe at her tears. *Don't think of the past. Concentrate on something else. Suz!* She was supposedly with Tyler but that fact wasn't reassuring.

She glanced at the trio behind her. "Chief Ballard is aware of my situation, Officer. Nash, I don't know where Suz went. She wasn't home when I arrived. All I found was a note that she'd be back soon, but she's not answering her cell phone. Whoever did this must know when she's around. I'm worried about her."

"We'll find her." Nash squeezed Ela's arm. "Officer, you should contact Chief Ballard and put out a BOLO for Suz Danforth."

When the patrolman didn't answer, Ela pleaded, "Please, my sister might be in danger."

CHAPTER 10

The bubble of panic expanded in Ela's chest. "Please, Officer, I haven't seen my sister since seven this morning."

"Ballard is here," Nash said as he stepped away from the parlor window.

In minutes, the Chief was inside. "Good evening, Miss Danforth. McCain, you keep turning up like a bad case of heartburn."

"And you're the sunshine of my life."

The men's hostility ratcheted up the strain in the room.

Office Greene stepped forward. "A video camera outside captured the trespasser, but the quality is poor. Chances are slim our techie can improve it."

"Bag the tape for us. What's happening, Miss Danforth?"

"My sister is missing. You'll need to turn on the Amber Alert. I'll get her picture for you." Ela didn't wait for his approval.

She brushed past Nash aware he kept his gaze on her as she left the room. What a night. She flicked on the light in the paneled office and yanked out the drawer with the photos. Most of them were old, but all she needed was one with a strong resemblance. She sifted through stationery, pens and pads of paper while a memory pushed into her consciousness.

"I sent the family our engagement photo." Aaron had laid the newspaper down on the coffee table in his living room. "Ray wrote that he's jealous because I'm marrying the most beautiful woman in the world. He plans to fly in from California a few days before the wedding to enjoy a little alone time with us."

"Now I feel pressure to look like a model." Ela ran her fingers through her tangled hair and fought the impulse to run from the couch to the nearest mirror. "I hope we won't need your brother to negotiate peace for family arguments over the wedding."

Aaron sat down beside her on the leather couch and rested his palm on her knee. "He gives discounts to family and friends."

"I'm serious, Aaron."

"You'll do fine. On another note, the Judge consented to officiate at our ceremony."

"But I always wanted a church—"

"I'll take care of everything. Don't worry."

Don't worry. Don't worry. Ela took a deep breath to refocus herself and dug out a brown leather album from Aunt Vickie's desk. She paged through it without success. On the bookshelf, she spotted another album and began leafing through it. The video must hold a clue. She stopped hunting through the pages and mentally rewound and played the tape. The image of the man in the hoodie froze in her mind. Something was familiar. She set the scene free in her thoughts and discovered a two-year-old snapshot of Suz and removed it from the plastic cover.

Photo in hand, she rushed into the parlor. Only Ballard and Nash were there.

"My men can use the picture but I can't guarantee an Amber Alert since your sister's hasn't been missing—"

Shouts from outside penetrated the walls of the house.

"Suz?" Ela darted by the two men and out into the rain.

Tyler's car was in the driveway. The officer was arguing with him and Suz.

Ela charged past the lawman and hugged her sister.

"I wasn't gone that long. You're embarrassing me." Suz broke free. "You're embarrassing yourself. Why are the police here?" She raised her chin and glared at her sister. "Did they come for Tyler?"

"I called them because I thought something happened to you."

Tyler wrapped an arm around Suz's waist. "We went to the diner."

"We had a lot to discuss, and I didn't know I was on the

clock." Suz leaned into Tyler. "I'm not calling to announce how long I chew my food." She wiped water from her dripping forehead and faced the officer. "Hello, it's raining. Can we go in the house?"

Suz was home. Ela couldn't stop the smile of relief spreading across her face.

Before they reached the house, Chief Ballard appeared and barred their way. "Hold it, young lady. Were you detained by anyone tonight?"

"Only by bad service at the diner. I admit it should be a crime."

Tyler snickered.

"This is serious. Your sister believed you were kidnapped or worse. At first glance, this mannequin on the lawn looked like you. Next time, phone her. Officers, finish up."

Suz wrinkled her nose at the dummy. "I don't look anything like that thing. Her hair's a mess, and she's naked. Ewww."

Ela hooked an arm around her sister's shoulders. "Let's go inside."

"Weird. Never mind everyone wants to know where I am day and night," Suz grumbled under her breath as they walked onto the porch.

"It happens when you're loved," Nash advised.

"I don't get why the cops came because we took a while to eat." Tyler scratched his head.

"Yeah, Ela, what's going on?" Suz demanded, wriggling free from her sister.

"I'll tell you once we're out of the rain."

In the parlor, Ela filled them in on the story about the dummy. Nash stood by the window and watched the officers outside. She finished talking and paused for her sister to apologize. When Suz remained mute, Ela gave her a pointed look. "Don't you want to say something?"

"You called a lawyer?" Suz tipped her head at Nash walking toward them. "Did you think they'd accuse you of kidnapping me?"

"Your sister's been frantic to find you," Nash said, joining them.

"El, if you wanted to call the police over the weird dummy,

okay, but you can't go off the deep end if I'm not here at the exact moment you expected me." She sank onto the sofa.

Ela's blood pressure shot up. To distract herself she asked Nash if Ballard and his men had left.

"They just did," he said. "They carried mini Suz off with them."

Suz jumped forward on the settee. "What about the camera? We can watch the video and see who used our yard for a landfill."

"Ballard confiscated the tape while you were outside," Nash informed them.

"I've got it!" Ela shouted as the image popped into her head. "I know who dumped the dummy. It was Mr. Brown from SOC."

"Socks?" Suz asked. "Someone who works in a department store is trying to scare you?"

"They're a protest group," Nash explained. "They demonstrate against unsafe roads in Rockypoint, especially Dead Man's Curve. Why do you think it's the man from the hospital, Ela?"

"I've been replaying the video in my mind, and noticed he walked oddly. Mr. Socks dragged his right foot slightly when he ran into the parking lot."

"You met him?" Suz wrinkled her nose.

"He grabbed me outside the emergency entrance the day I went to bring you home. He rushed off when Nash showed up."

"Grabbed you!" Suz shuddered. "He sounds dangerous."

"Yeah, the cops love arresting people," Tyler said. "They should catch him right away."

Nash dug out his cell phone from his pocket.

"Who are you calling?" Ela asked.

"Ballard, to tell him you ID'd the man in the video and can give him a detailed description."

"You should have mentioned someone assaulted you at the hospital, El," Suz's voice held a note of sympathy. "I would have understood why you were late picking me up."

Her sister's tone brought a rush of pleasure to Ela. "My goal was to bring you home, not frighten you, and he didn't assault me."

Suz jiggled the foot of her crossed leg up and down. "They

should throw the lowlife in jail and lose the key. Then they can stop harassing Tyler."

"Before Ballard and I have a conversation," Nash interjected, "Suz, how about sitting for Lanie on Saturday? Does that fit your schedule and Ela's?"

"Yesss." Suz traded a glance with Tyler.

"You're discussing babysitting now?" Why were they having a casual conversation when she might have figured out who was harassing them?

"Suz, tell your sister while I use my phone." Nash walked into the other room with his cell to his ear.

"I'm going to babysit Lanie, and Nash is going to represent Tyler."

What was she talking about? "Was Tyler arrested?"

"No, Nash is our safety hatch. You always remind me to plan ahead. He will be our lawyer, our go to man."

She'd like Nash to be her man, too. Ela's thoughts jumped back to their embrace on the porch, his strong arms around her, and the scent of leather. Okay, she was attracted to him. But she could ignore the signals and keep a safe distance between them. She had enough problems without adding another man into the mix.

"Okay, Ela? Ela?" Suz waved a hand in front of Ela's eyes.

"Okay." Wait, had she just agreed to the whole lopsided idea of exchanging sitting for a lawyer's services? She stifled the urge to argue. If Nash kept an eye on Tyler's activities, at least Suz would be safer.

"Ballard wants to meet downtown," Nash said, returning to the parlor.

"I'm ready, Nash. Suz. We'll talk later."

* * *

The next morning, the sun peeked under the bedroom shades and promised to shine all day. Ela pulled the sheet over her head for another few minutes of sleep. She'd spent three hours at the station searching through pictures to ID Mr. Soc. When she failed to find him, Ela worked with a sketch artist to produce a likeness.

Chief Ballard took the finished product and gave his word to track down the new suspect. At last she'd learn why Mr. Soc or Brown was terrorizing them.

After breakfast, she showered, dressed in navy pants and a light blue blouse and left for work at the two-story brick library. The work day passed without incident, and she hiked to Aunt Vickie's shop before dark to continue her inventory.

She was half a block away from Now and Then when impulse struck. She detoured down a side street to the modest stone chapel she'd spied from the corner. A wooden Welcome sign on the patch of green grass beckoned her forward.

She entered through the arched wooden doors and sat in the last row of the empty church. The scarred overhead beams and tall wooden pews gave a sense of another time. A vase of crimson and white carnations stood at the end of the aisle as though someone had dropped them off. Unlit candles and a cross mounted behind the altar decorated the front of the house of worship.

Light streamed through tall, narrow windows and shone over the altar. She sat soaking in the silence and peace. The fragrance of the flowers reminded her of the first days of spring when she walked through Central Park and enjoyed the tulips and daffodils. She closed her eyes and exhaled her stress.

The fall of footsteps announced another's presence. An elderly man with a cane joined her on the church bench. He put the stick aside. His shoulders in the plaid jacket hunched forward in prayer for several seconds before he raised his head. His eyes widened as he swept his gaze over her. "My daughter's hair looked exactly like yours."

Ela nodded, at a loss for the right words.

"She's gone now. I'd give anything to see her one more time." His mouth turned downward for a brief second before he stretched out his gnarled hand for the cane that had slid to the floor between them.

The memory of her father bending to kiss her goodbye every morning before he left flashed through her mind. "I want to go to work with you, Dad," she told him one day.

"When you're older, we'll work together." He tugged on her braid and smiled.

"Pardon me. I can't quite reach it."

The old man's words brought Ela into the present. She retrieved his cane and passed it to him.

"You made my day, Miss." The man rose and hobbled away.

The click of the chapel door told her he'd left. A wave of grief passed over her. Since the age of six, she'd planned to join her father at his office. But, she'd lost the father she knew forever. She wiped the tears from the corners of her eyes.

The sun's rays slanted downward onto the benches. She needed to get to the shop. Outside, she hurried on her way and found no sign of the senior on the sidewalk.

Ten minutes later, she arrived at Now and Then and started work on the inventory to help her forget her father. She began with the old metal trunk in the rear. Opening it, she expected the odor of mothballs to permeate the air. Instead, the hint of lavender perfume clung to the layers of embroidered handkerchiefs inside. Underneath, she found several collections of old postcards. The breathtaking picture of a setting sun in hues of red and gold caught her attention. She flipped over the card. It was addressed to Aunt Vickie. Ela read the message: *Soon, every sunset will be ours. Forever yours, Roy.*

Roy had been Aunt Vickie's boyfriend in college. Ela's mother often talked about how Aunt Vickie had put off marriage to establish her business, and Roy grew tired of the delays and married someone else. Mom believed Aunt Vickie secretly regretted her choice, but after his engagement was announced, she never mentioned him again.

Ela stuck the postcard in her notebook with the inventory. The squeak of the door announced the arrival of an attractive, older woman with short, fluffy, white hair. She wore a simple, crimson dress and shot Ela a fleeting polite smile. "You must be the new owner. I have heard a lot about you."

Ela grabbed the pad of paper and moved to the counter. "I'm sorry. We're no longer open. I should have locked up." The woman's last words sank in. "Did I hear you say you've heard a lot about me?"

Her visitor wove between the stacks of furniture, silver bracelets jingling. "Yes, you know my son, Nashua. I'm Margaret McCain." She paused and held out a hand.

Surprised, Ela accepted the handshake. Margaret's grip was firm, and her stare roamed over Ela's face.

Ela had the uneasy feeling she was checking her out.

"I don't know your son well," she said pointedly.

"Oh, Nash is easy to know. He isn't a game player, except in the courtroom. He's a natural born lawyer, like his father." Margaret moved aside to study a Wedgewood vase on the glass display case. "You've tons of interesting items."

"Were you a friend of my Aunt Vickie?"

"We knew each other through her business, not on a personal level, but she always was friendly and a delight to deal with. She loved her store. I can't wait until you reopen. I have several friends who loved the shop, too." The older woman pivoted around taking in the store's contents.

"You misunderstood. I'm not reopening Now and Then. I'm liquidating it."

"Oh, dear, I'm sad to hear that." Her sharp hazel focused on Ela. "I hope you hired a first class realtor."

"I did, but I'm having an estate sale before I list the building. You should come and bring your friends. I'm sure you'll find something to buy. I'm targeting next month."

"Thanks for the tip. I'll spread the word. In fact, I have the name of the best woman to manage your sale. She sets up, advertises and has connections to the other shops and dealers in the area."

"Do you have her contact information?" A huge weight lifted from Ela's shoulders. "I'd love to hire someone I can trust."

"I'll get her number tonight. Here's mine." Mrs. McCain dug in her purse for a pen. "Call me tomorrow."

Ela opened up her notebook and laid it on the counter. "Please, write it on the inside of the cover, Mrs. McCain."

"I'm Margaret. She poised the pen above the book, wrote and then straightened. "I know what makes sense. Join us for dinner on Sunday, and we'll discuss the sale."

A ping of worry shot through Ela's chest. "I couldn't intrude on your weekend, and I just met Nash. I mean it's almost like inviting a stranger. My sister and I haven't lived in town long." She sounded idiotic, stringing one excuse after the other.

"All the more reason for you both to come, so no one will be left alone." Margaret's jaw jutted out in a stubborn line. "I won't take no for an answer, and living in Rockypoint is about being neighborly." She dropped the pen into her purse. "I love antiques, the excitement of sale day, and I'm positive you'll enjoy our dinner, too." She gave a firm nod and walked to the door.

"I don't know your address."

Margaret turned around. "Nash will pick you up at two, and I cook a large meal every Sunday. It's no bother. Bye, dear." The door shut with the protest of the hinges. Nash's mother pulled away in the red hybrid parked at the curb.

The woman had just railroaded her into dinner. What would Nash think of Ela, intruding into their lives? He'd think she was looking for more in their relationship.

She'd call and cancel. A small jolt of disappointment settled in her stomach. What was wrong with her? She couldn't get involved with Nash and his family. She hadn't met Aaron's mother until after the engagement. Aaron had been at her apartment, seated on her sofa the day they were to arrive.

Ela was searching for the right dress to wear and held up a periwinkle one that reached past her knees. "Should I wear this dress?"

"Is that for a pioneer?"

She tossed it on the beige barrel chair. "You're right. Only Laura Ingalls would wear it." His parents would expect a princess after Aaron's buildup. Her anxiety wound higher.

He stood and rested his hands on her shoulders. "My parents are going to love you because I do."

She shot him an exasperated look. "Clichéd answer, but smart."

He smiled and lowered his lips to hers.

His image faded away with the beep of a horn on the street.

Her gaze fell on the postcard sticking out of the notebook. Aunt Vickie hadn't taken a chance on Roy and regretted it her entire life. What if Nash, not Aaron, was her Roy?

CHAPTER 11

The April sun hid while the week crawled to Sunday morning. Ela drew open the parlor blackout curtains that she'd spent her sleepless nights sewing.

When she'd lived in New York, she'd have been dressed and ready for church by now. She closed her eyes and imagined the flicker of lit candles, the scent of dripping wax. Nothing else compared to that feeling of belonging among her friends and fellow members. The pain of loss struck her, and she blinked against the tears.

The parlor phone rang, and she picked it up. Chief Ballard wasted no time informing her that the police techie couldn't improve the quality of the surveillance video from her porch. His investigators had yet to locate and question the man who'd approached her at the hospital.

"The SOC group claimed he's not a member," the chief told her. "He's not related to the victims' families either."

"How do we learn his identity?"

"We've the sketch drawn from your description, and we're going through the DMV pictures for a facial match. Then we'll try the National Data Bank. We'll get him, no matter where he's hiding."

A dozen reasons why they wouldn't locate him scrolled through her head. She pushed them aside. "You think it's someone from our past?"

"I think we look everywhere until we ID him."

"Thanks for the update."

"Keep your sister close. Don't let her go out alone." Ballard ended the call.

Suz would love his advice. Yesterday, when her sister had sat for Lanie, Ela had checked in every half hour.

Suz had followed the calls with three texts: "I'm alive. Still breathing. Stop the mother smother."

The thump of her sister's crutches interrupted Ela's musings. She hung up the parlor phone as Suz swung into the room.

She halted and scanned Ela. "Are you wearing that to the big dinner?"

Ela ran a hand over her silk blouse. "Is something wrong?"

"Of course not, if you want Nash's family to think you work in a morgue or you're a member of the Addams Family."

"At least I'm stylish somewhere. Chief Ballard called and recommended you not go anywhere alone."

"I'm never alone. Tyler drives me to school and back, and Tyler or you are here after classes. When I sat with Lanie, you called every minute."

"I worry about you."

"Stress is bad for your health. Every therapist talks about it. Ela, did you know Lanie spends her Saturdays with her grandmother? She never goes to a friend's house." Suz wrinkled her nose. "Maybe the whole family keeps women prisoners. You'd better watch out for Nash."

"Lanie's nine, Suz. She's not running for Miss Congeniality. And Nash has nothing to do with my day-to-day activities."

"Come on, Ela. He's into you, and I still think Lanie spending her free time with her family is strange. I went to lots of friends' houses when I was her age."

"Mom probably dropped you off and ran for her life."

"Funny. By the way, I was invited to the McCains' dinner today, along with you."

"Where did you meet Margaret McCain?"

"I didn't. Lanie asked me after we put a hole in the lampshade in their living room."

"Are you kidding? Did you pay for it?" *Suz* needed a sitter.

Her sister balanced for a second on one foot, rested the crutches against the settee and collapsed on the cushion. "Don't worry. I told Lanie I'd replace it, but she hatched a better idea. The girl's got a bright future."

"I hope you're not suggesting as a liar."

Suz rolled her eyes.

Ela was getting caught in Suz's teen drama. *React calmly.* "You should tell Nash about the lamp if he doesn't know. Are you coming to the McCain's? You can be responsible and confess before we eat."

"I'm not going with you. Tyler has the day off, and Lanie worked out the lamp thing. She stuck a Red Sox sticker over the tear. It was an improvement. The shade was yucky tan." Suz snatched a magazine from the coffee table.

"You'll lose your sitting job. Why did you throw a ball inside the house in the first place?"

"Relax. Lanie and I confessed when Nash came home and he loved the lampshade. He was cool with the whole ball—in—the—living—room scene."

"I can't believe you didn't use better judgment." Her sister had never gotten into trouble in school, but outside of class she seemed to lose IQ points.

"I only told you in case Nash brought up the accident at dinner. Do we have anything good in the refrigerator?"

"We've plenty of leftovers. And use those functioning brain cells when you're babysitting. Are you sure you don't want to come with me to dinner?"

"Why do you want me to tag along on your date?"

"It's not a date."

"Ela, think back a hundred years when you had a life. A guy picks you up in a car and takes you to his parents' house. What do we call it?"

"His mother invited me."

"I'd guess because her son has been talking about you, and she decided to meet you. And, you should go out with him. He's hot." She stood up and settled her crutches under her arms.

"I'm relieved to have your approval." Despite her joking words, Suz's statement set free a cluster of butterflies in Ela's stomach. "What are the odds of you and Tyler staying in?"

"We're going to look at apartments."

"Suz, are you still considering moving in together? I won't consent."

"Relax. It's for Tyler and his friend, Dylan. I told them I can't afford to move out." She held up her hand. "I'm staying with you, for now."

Her answer wasn't quite what Ela wanted, but she didn't want to push the issue.

At the sound of an engine in the drive, Suz hopped around on her crutches to the window. "Your date's early."

"Thanks, Suz." Ela toyed with the button on her blouse. She wanted to make a good impression. Margaret McCain had offered to help her, and outside of Margaret and her son, no one else had offered her a hand in ages. "But this is not a date."

Why was she even paying attention to her sister? She wasn't an expert on relationships. She dated Tyler!

The doorbell rang. Ela strode across the room, aware that Suz watched her. She and Nash were just friends. Just friends. Ela opened the door.

He stood in front of her in khakis and a sea green shirt that brought out the flecks of jade in his hazel eyes. "Hi, you look great. Ready to go?" He flashed a wider smile that would win over a hung jury. For a brief moment, she lost the power of speech.

What was wrong with her? She dipped her head, breaking eye contact and cleared her throat. "Let me get my jacket. It's...in the coat closet." She yanked the garment off the hanger and turned around to his open hands.

He took the jacket from her and held it up. "Is your sister coming? Lanie told me she invited her."

"Did I hear you talking about me?" Suz appeared in the hall. A smirk crossed her face as Nash finished settling the jacket on Ela's shoulders.

Ignore her. "My sister has plans with Tyler."

"Thanks for yesterday," Nash said to Suz. "You were a big hit. Lanie asked if I'd work next weekend so you could come over again."

"Sure." Suz beamed smugly at her sister.

Ela turned to the door. Her stomach continued doing flip flops. Ridiculous. She wasn't on a first date. She'd gone out with other men before Aaron.

Aaron...

The recollection of the dinner that changed his life edged into her consciousness. After work, the three of them escaped to the little French restaurant he loved. Her father had held up his glass of champagne. "Excuse an old line, but I couldn't be happier about my daughter's forthcoming marriage and I've an announcement. I'd like to offer my new son-in-law a permanent position in our firm. We've grown huge in the last year and need a full time lawyer on board. Say yes, and you begin Monday."

"You better get going so everything stays *hot*," Suz urged.

At the sound of her sister's voice, Ela crashed back into the present and glanced at her hot, hot date.

* * *

Nash drove for ten minutes across town to a neighborhood of homes with perfectly manicured lawns. The McCains owned a large, two-story gray house with black shutters set back from the road. Lanie and Nash's parents politely greeted her at the door before Lanie and her grandfather settled at the coffee table to play a rousing pre-dinner game of Chinese checkers.

With Nash at her elbow, Margaret gave Ela a tour of her house, which on the outside, appeared unassuming, but inside was ready for a photo shoot by Perfect Country Homes Magazine. Ela guessed the furniture pieces and accessories were antiques and not reproductions.

Margaret's pride in her house led Ela to believe she was a homebody, but her polite and sharp questions regarding Ela's past left her uneasy, as though she were standing trial. She answered basic queries such as where she'd lived and worked, but when Margaret started to quiz Ela about family, Nash stepped in and changed the conversation. Ela's discomfort caused her palms to dampen, and her eagerness to get dinner over grew. Everyone better be a speed eater, she thought.

They sat in the formal living room while Margaret listed the names of the people who'd already promised to attend Ela's estate sale and gave her the history of each person's buying habits. By meal time, her nerves had subsided, and the afternoon reached the homestretch.

So far, Margaret McCain had proven a mix of Attila the Hun, a criminal investigator and a wise TV mother. Ela sat across from Nash in the dining room. An antique ivory tablecloth warned that spills would be obvious and kept as evidence of any clumsiness on her part. She pushed the chair as close to the table as she could to close the gap between herself and her plate.

"Dad, would you do the honors?" Margaret asked Simon.

Ela bent her head as her host's firm voice asked for a blessing and added a thank you for sending Ela to their table. A rush of pleasure accompanied an ache of longing to belong to a family. Nash raised his head, catching her attention, and winked. She quickly glanced away.

When they finished the blessing, Margaret spoke first from her place at one end of the table. "I understand your sister babysat for Lanie the other day." Margaret smiled at her granddaughter, seated next to Nash.

"I like her," Lanie said. "She's fun. May I have more gravy, Grandma?"

"Yes, you may."

"Do you enjoy baseball?" Simon McCain asked her. "Nash, you should take Ela to a Red Sox game. We've box seats at Fenway, and they're playing the Yankees next week."

"If you don't mind me cheering for the Yankees."

"Speaking of baseball," Nash interjected before his father recovered from the shocked look of having a Yankee fan at the table. "Lanie and Suz pitched a few yesterday. Lanie hit a lamp with my autographed baseball."

"She fixed it," Ela blurted. An awkward silence settled over the table. Why had she yelled out? This was a disaster.

Simon broke the moment by laying his fork on his plate with a clang "Lanie, you threw a ball?"

Lanie hung her head.

"You threw it at a lamp?" Margaret asked. "Why would you do such a thing?"

"We were looking at Dad's baseball with the autographs, and Suz said she'd show me how to pitch." Lanie kept her gaze on her plate. "I wanted to throw it first, and the lamp was in the way, but it works fine." She raised her head. "The ball made a tiny hole in the shade. You can't even see it. Right, Dad?"

"I did mention tossing a ball might be fun before I left. The

Red Sox decal over the rip fixed the tear, but her pitching days in the house are done."

Simon chuckled. "She should take up home decorating. I'd appreciate a Red Sox lamp."

"I have never known Lanie to break anything." Margaret blinked several times. "She's always been…"

"Perfect?" Nash offered.

"She's still perfect," Simon winked at his granddaughter. "Lanie, why don't you pour another helping of gravy?"

"Thanks, Grandpa." Lanie scooped up the gravy dish and drowned her potatoes.

"Does your sister play ball, Ela?" Simon asked.

"No, she was into dance. Now she's into boys." Oh, oh, that sounded bad. "She's really a good kid."

"I'm sure she's lovely," Margaret said in a voice that sounded as though she meant the opposite.

"Some days," Ela admitted. Some days long, long ago.

"Being new in Rockypoint must be difficult for her. Teenagers always need good role models. Your sister should join one of the high school clubs." Margaret rested her fork on her plate. "Nash, you should bring Ela and her sister to church next week and introduce them. We've an active women's organization you might—"

"Thank you, but I work at the shop on Sunday."

"Surely, you can take a few—"

"Mom," Nash interrupted, "remember the constitution and freedom of worship."

Margaret folded her hands in front of her. "I was trying to acquaint Ela with our town."

Ela forced a smile. "Mrs. McCain, you've done enough by including me in your family dinner and helping spread the word about my estate sale."

Nash laid a hand on his mother's arm. "You've chosen the right woman to put out your news."

Mrs. McCain's tight expression eased. "Thank you, Ela. Since everyone has finished eating, I'll bring out the dessert." Margaret rose. "Lanie, you can help me."

Ela pushed to her feet. "None for me. The food was

delicious, but I should go home. My sister gets nervous when she stays alone for long."

"I thought Nash told me she had company," Margaret protested.

"She did, but I'm sure he's gone by now." Ela hoped she wasn't struck by lightning for her lie.

Margaret opened her mouth to object when Nash stood and cut her off. "I'll get your jacket."

Within minutes, Ela thanked her hosts and finally relaxed when she clicked on the seatbelt in Nash's sports car.

"Sorry if my mother came on strong. She means well, but she's never understood that people don't want others butting into their business."

Ela tossed the next thought around in her mind and decided to confess. "We're not alike, your mom and I."

"I'm not looking for a twin."

"I bet she's the model in the community. Nash, my father's in prison." She rushed on, letting her feelings pour out. "He defrauded the people who trusted him. He ruined lives. I was engaged to a man who couldn't face the justice system and died because of it. My mother escaped to another country. I was investigated for fraud and cleared, but that doesn't inspire confidence. I'm sure your mother would prefer you bring someone respectable to her dinner table."

"Respectable? Are you kidding me? If you shake our family tree, all the people hiding from the law will fall out. My great, great uncle isn't even on a branch unless you count the one they hanged him from for horse thievery."

He paused, then continued when she didn't respond. "Ela, we're human. We all have things we wish were different in our heritage."

"Most folks don't change their name to escape connections to their father. Your horse thief is now a tale from long ago. It's not quite comparable, but thanks for letting me in on your family secrets and trying to make me feel better."

They traveled in silence until Nash braked for a stoplight. "I'll speak to my mother. She came on a little strong because she's not used to me bringing a date to dinner."

He'd said the word: date. Suz was right. "You don't need to

apologize. She was being your mother. I can imagine how mine would have acted if I brought you home."

"You've a unique way of complimenting me, Danforth."

"That's why all the men swarm around me. Seriously—"

"I was being serious."

"Thanks. I would give anything to have my mother in Rockypoint, sitting at the table, making me uncomfortable. Suz and I miss her every day, and wish she'd come home. Enjoy your mom."

"No one's ever told me to enjoy time with my mother." He pulled into her driveway and cut the engine.

Don't sit here. Jump out of the car. She grabbed the handle.

"Wait."

"What is it?"

"I like you, Ela Danforth." He tucked a curl behind her ear. "You're fair and care about people."

Her skin warmed where his hand brushed across her skin. He leaned closer. *Thank him and tell him you don't feel the same. Tell him you're exhausted. Tell him anything, but don't kiss him.*

She closed her eyes. Their lips met. His mouth was firm and strong against hers. She gripped his shoulders. His hands dove into her hair, pulling her head closer, and lingered. The long, slow kiss clouded her mind. What was she supposed to do? Oh, yes, leave. She tilted her head away. "Nash?"

"Hmm." His kisses wandered across her cheekbones and her eyelids leaving her skin tingling before he broke away. "Ela, I don't just like you."

Huh? Her mind cleared. Perfect ending for an almost date.

"I like you a lot, Ela."

She scooped up her purse from the floorboards to give herself time to figure out an answer. She had to set him straight.

The door handle felt firm in her hand. "I like you, too." The words flowing out of her mouth sounded slick and fake.

The glow left his eyes. She sensed his disappointment.

She pointed toward the car in front of them to change the subject. "Tyler is here. He and Suz must be wondering what's taking me so long to come inside."

"I doubt they're wondering." A grin spread across his face.

Worse and worse. She pushed down on the handle. "Thanks for dinner."

He frowned. "Your sister told me you've a grudge against lawyers because your father's legal deal went south."

"Suz talks too much." Her sister should learn that silence is golden and would earn her points.

"Give me your version of the experience. I want to understand."

Ela released the handle. The depth of her father's dishonesty might give a lawyer second thoughts about a relationship with her. "After his arrest for fraud, my father hired a dream team for his defense. As the trial went on, his fate grew grimmer and his money dwindled. His attorneys fled the sinking ship, except for one who explained that my father's only hope was to plead. He predicted the judge would give my father ten years. With good behavior, he'd be released in the near future and have a life left. His lawyer assured my father it was a good deal and my dad agreed."

"I'll guess what happened next. The judge threw him a curve ball."

She nodded. "My dad was sentenced to fifty years. He'll never be released. Now you know." She hopped out and bent down to add, "The worst part was I encouraged him to take the plea bargain. But at least, he can't hurt anyone again." As she shut the door, she spotted her elderly neighbor at her window staring out at her. Double great.

Ela marched toward the porch. From behind came the sound of Nash's footsteps.

Suz dashed onto the porch and folded her arms over her chest. "You're late, Miss Danforth. It's almost four thirty. What do you have to say for yourself, young lady?"

"You're not funny, Suz."

Suz turned to Nash. "Did you have a good dinner?"

"I'm glad you're back," Ela said before Nash could answer. "Is Tyler with you?"

"I was finishing my brownie" Tyler stepped out beside Suz. "We didn't get a chance to grab a bite when we were out."

"Glad you ate a healthy lunch." Ela walked inside and halted at the sight of the brown wrapped package on the hall table. Her name and address were printed in large block letters across the paper.

Nash entered with Tyler and Suz who were quizzing him on the dinner. He paused next to Ela, and his gaze fell on her mail. "A Sunday delivery must have cost someone a few dollars."

"Are you going to open it, El?" Suz poked her arm.

Ela drew her chin upward. "Throw it out."

Her cell phone rang from inside her purse in the stunned silence. She dug it out. She didn't need the ID to know who was on the other end. The phone call and gift were from *him*.

She pressed the button and burst into her speech. "Stop buying me gifts. I won't change my mind, and you don't want me to let the authorities know about your calls. So give it up before they trace them, and we'll both be winners."

Shaking, she hung up.

CHAPTER 12

Nash waited for Ela to explain the call. Instead, she ran a hand through her hair and complained about annoying telemarketers. An uncomfortable silence filled the entry.

Finally, he reached for the package. If she didn't want to tell him who called or sent her the brown wrapped gift, she didn't have to. "I'll do the honors, if you're frightened that—"

"No." Ela grabbed his arm, stopping him.

What was going on? He'd try another approach. "We can call Ballard. He'll take care of this if you're afraid the SOC protestor mailed it."

"Suz told me you carry a gun." Tyler's eyes gleamed. "Why don't you take the mail into the yard and shoot it? See if it blows up."

Suz nudged him to be quiet while she kept her gaze glued to Ela's face.

Ela and Suz seemed to know who sent the package, he thought.

"We don't need the police. I'll take care of it." Ela stretched out her hand.

Nash edged in front of her. "Do you know what's in it?"

"I recognize the writing, and I've a guess about the contents. Believe me, nothing will blow up. We're safe, physically."

"I'll put it in the trash I noticed in the garage." Nash held out his hands.

Suz leaned forward. "Tyler will take it out."

"Uh, sure. I hope you're right and your junk mail's not a bomb." He carried the gift in extended arms while Ela held the door for him, and Suz tailed him outside.

Then Ela faced Nash. "I don't want to keep you."

"I have time for a cup of coffee since we missed dessert." What was she hiding? He'd a few more questions for Ela Danforth.

"All right, come on." She led him into the other room. "You have to trust me," she said over her shoulder. "The parcel was nothing we want in our house." In the kitchen, she inserted the K-cup and hit the button.

"I'd like you to be up front. Is there someone else, such as an unwelcome boyfriend in your life? Was there someone before or after Aaron?" Was the package from an unwanted admirer turned stalker?

Her mouth fell open, and then she regained her composure. "No one fits the description, but since you've asked about boyfriends, sit down and I'll explain more about Aaron."

He sat while she put out cream and sugar and brought two cups of coffee to the table before easing into the seat next to him.

She gripped her hands around the mug in a clench. "When Aaron and I announced we were getting married, my dad was thrilled. Aaron was the son he always wanted and my father thought the stock market rose and fell with him." She tapped a finger on the handle of her cup. "At the time, I agreed. We were an ideal couple, but we broke up after my father was arrested."

"Why did you end it?"

"He couldn't deal with the press hounding him when word leaked my father was suspected of embezzling clients' funds. Watching Aaron under pressure, I realized he and I weren't the match I'd hoped." She drew in a ragged breath, and pain glimmered in her eyes.

"I'm sorry," he murmured, wishing sympathy could end her hurt.

"In the end, it was the right decision. Our stress levels shot into the red zone the day my father was indicted, and the media labeled us all guilty. The new DA began circling us and investigating everyone in our firm. I was cleared, but Aaron became entangled in a disappearing fund that he'd advised my father on. I don't believe he was innocent. My father was the embezzler."

Not finding the right words, Nash nodded for her to continue.

"People who were our friends turned against us. They treated me like Satan's daughter and Aaron like he murdered little children and puppies while they slept. He couldn't handle the hate, and he holed up in his apartment." She clenched her hands on the table and lowered her voice. "The hate was difficult for all of us."

He laid his palm over her fists. She didn't relax, but she didn't pull away. "I'm sorry, Ela. I wish I'd been there to help you."

"No one could. Aaron wanted out, but there was no out for him. His lawyer learned that a grand jury was about to charge him for co-conspiracy of fraud. Aaron told me he'd never overcome the stain on his legal career even though he was innocent."

"You believed he was blameless?"

"He was still learning the business. I don't think he'd have been able to fleece our customers when he'd just entered the firm. My father swore under oath that he acted alone and started stealing, small amounts at first, years before Aaron joined us. I've no reason to doubt my father."

"It must have been confusing for you."

"It was as bad for Aaron. The public was condemning him." Her shoulders sank downward, and the lines around her mouth deepened.

He encircled her hands with both his own.

She dipped her head and continued, "Aaron's parents had mortgaged their home and hired a team of lawyers to protect him when my father was indicted. The Judge knew the legal system required precautions. We ended our engagement, but we hadn't announced the breakup to his parents or brother. 'A family sticks together, especially when in trouble' was the Judge's motto, and they had considered me one of them. But I guess we no longer need to stick. Aaron's memorial was the last time we spoke." She locked her gaze on Nash. "Now you can understand why I avoid talking about Aaron. I've too many what ifs in my head."

"But your ex is sending you unwanted gifts and calling you." Unless there was another man in her life she refused to acknowledge. "Aaron's angry that you have a life and he doesn't." Unexpected resentment flared inside of him. How big an idiot was the man?

"What? No." Distress roughened her voice. "I told you. He's dead. He died during the whole mess in New York. Aaron's not calling. She averted her gaze.

What was she hiding? All his instincts pointed to a woman covering for a man.

"Tyler and I are going out." Suz swung into the kitchen. She glanced at Ela's face and Nash's hand over hers. "What's going on?"

"We're talking." Ela scooted the chair away from the table, breaking their contact. She rose and walked to the refrigerator. "I was going to eat some ice cream. Want a dish?"

"That trick to keep me in hasn't worked since I was ten, Ela."

"Funny, it works for me," Nash said. "I'd love a scoop."

"Hey," Tyler shouted from the parlor. "Come quick."

Nash followed the women into the other room where Tyler was sitting on the settee. What was an emergency in his world?

"Watch this." Tyler pointed at the TV.

A blonde woman, who looked around twenty, read into the camera: "Local police are urging anyone in the North End Neighborhood to report unusual sightings or information they may have about this crime to the tip line."

Tyler muted the voice. "You missed the good part. Someone broke into a house, a street over from you. The home owner collected guns, and the thief stole two of them."

"I'm comforted by the news." Ela wrapped her arms around her waist.

"We should nail the windows shut." Suz gestured toward the front panes of glass. "Forget the blackout curtains we put up."

"Suz, we can't live in a coffin."

"Love the image, El." Suz crossed the floor and plopped beside Tyler.

"I'll protect you." Tyler puffed up his chest.

"Now we're really in trouble," Ela said. "Suz, don't open up for any more deliveries."

"Ela, you're so negative." Suz pushed out her lower lip.

"Everyone." Nash walked to the center of the room. "You're *safe*. Suz, I'm taking a wild guess you won't answer the door for any delivery men since you want to be extra cautious."

"I meant to send the guy with the package away, but he was cute and didn't act dangerous." She slid a peek at Tyler. "Not as cute as my boyfriend."

Nash glanced at his watch. He was surprised his mother hadn't phoned to ask what happened to him. "Ela, I'm sorry, but Lanie expects me at my parents' house. Since no one is in danger, I'll go. Rain check on the ice cream."

"I'll walk you out." She cut a quick look at Suz and Tyler who were whispering to each other on the settee.

In the hall, Nash halted. "I'll say goodbye here."

A startled look crossed her face. He threaded his fingers through hers and squeezed. "Lanie has school tomorrow." He released her to open the three locks. "Call if you need me before morning. Otherwise, we'll talk then." He touched her cheek and strode to his car, wishing he could stay longer.

At his parents, Nash fended off his mother's inquires and left with Lanie. Once they were at their house, Nash settled in the kitchen with his laptop to become fully versed on the life of Aaron Wright. From the living room came the mumbles of the TV, a reminder he needed to shut off the computer soon. He always ended their evening with a read aloud to Lanie.

He scrolled down the page of the last newspaper article on the screen:

After a two-year successful law career, Aaron Wright, a financial lawyer from California, accepted a position as a private attorney for the New York firm of Blanchette Financial.

Nash skimmed over the facts of Matt Blanchette's legal problems until he reached key information.

Wright was under investigation by the DA at the time he disappeared from his private yacht. His fiancée, Michaela Blanchette, reported that he was on a fishing trip from his vacation home in the Hamptons.

Rumors had spread that he was about to be arrested for co-conspiracy for financial fraud. Wright's disappearance at a crucial time raises many questions and suspicions, including the fact that he emptied his bank account before he vanished. The investigation into the Blanchette Financial Firm where Wright was employed is ongoing. Blanchette's daughter, Michaela, also worked for the firm, and continues to be under scrutiny.

"At least she escaped." Nash closed the article. Escaped to what? She was living in Rockypoint where a slimeball had forced her sister off Dead Man's Curve, was sending Ela unwanted gifts and violating the security of their home by watching them inside their house and most likely, cutting up their mother's picture.

The actions all appeared personal and vindictive. The coward had taken the easy way out and abandoned Ela to save himself. Now he wanted her attention and to punish her for making him an outcast. Ela held herself responsible for his problems, and he did, too.

Nash mentally brought up the image of Ela's pained face. Had she fallen out of love with her ex, or was she telling Nash and herself, a lie?

Nash would love to get Aaron Wright into a courtroom, but another idea flashed through his mind. Within minutes, he had set up the new website findaaronwright.com. He wrote a brief bio for the supposedly deceased man and invited others to leave tips or sightings of Aaron. Maybe he'd flush out a conspirator who had harbored Ela's ex-fiancé and regretted his actions.

Ela had told him not to waste money on a search for Aaron, and Nash had done as Ela wished. He contacted his techie to monitor the IP addresses of the computers that accessed the site. The techie drew a regular pay from their firm. No waste there.

The doorbell rang as he finished typing the last word. He rose and called to Lanie to stay put. He glanced through the narrow hall window at the familiar figure on his step before he opened up.

"Mr. Rawlings reporting to his lawyer." Tyler gave a salute.

"Come in and lock the door. You're just in time for a good book." When Tyler looked confused, Nash added, "Don't worry. It's painless and short. Follow me."

* * *

Money Bags had called him twice yesterday to moan and piss. Now he'd be happy. Soon there'd be one less person on the planet.

The rifles were perfect and better than his. He could sight the Danforth chick clear across the county. He laughed.

His phone rang. He grabbed it from his jeans pocket.

"Don't ever leave me a message. I call you. Understood?"

"Yeah, but you wanted to know how I was going to get her. I've got what I needed."

"Stolen guns? No way. They're too easy to trace. Do it the way we last discussed. Go off the plan again and our deal is over."

Money Bags wanted to act like the king boss. The rifles were a great idea. "I'll do it your way, but the price went up." He hit the off button. Let Money stress for a while. The guy deserved it.

His gaze fell on the gun lying on his lumpy couch. He sat down and stroked her cold body.

* * *

Night faded into morning, and the gray skies threatened rain. Ela carried her umbrella to work and spent the day stacking and organizing. At lunchtime, Suz texted her. She was hanging with Tyler after work. She'd be home later.

The temptation to shoot back a message demanding Suz's afternoon schedule warred with Ela's desire to keep her sister safe and the truth that Suz needed to live her life. Going home to an empty house seemed less appealing as the hour drew near. Of course, she could invite Nash over for a visit. No, he had to work.

Outside, Ela detoured to Now and Then. She'd finish up her inventory and call the realtor to green-light the store's sale.

The weather showed no improvement from the morning. She kept up a brisk pace as she strode to the street where the antique shop sat dark and locked. Customers browsed through the tattoo parlor on the corner and the used bookstore windows. At least she wasn't alone. She searched the road for the navy sedan, but it was nowhere in sight.

Unlocking the door, she reached in and flipped the light switch. The piles of furniture and collectibles were still there. Where were the antique elves that would set up the showrooms at night? She set her purse on the shelf under the counter and pulled out the notebook with her working list.

Her phone rang. Checking the ID, she found her realtor's number in the cell's window. No sense putting him off. "Hello, Kevin. I bet you're calling about the contract. I'll sign it, but I'm having an estate sale first."

"I can recommend a woman I've worked with before."

"I have someone, and I'm at the store if you want to come by, or you can email the paperwork to my home if you're tied up. I don't have a computer here. I gotta go." She disconnected before he answered. An ache cramped her stomach. Tears blurred her vision. "I'm sorry, Aunt Vickie. If I could keep Now and Then, I would, but I have to pay off Suz's hospital bill, the storage rentals with your other antiques and the taxes. You get it."

She climbed to the second floor loft, but couldn't shake the sensation that her aunt's spirit wanted to voice her disappointment that Ela had failed and was selling off her aunt's dream.

Ela hesitated at the top of the steps, and tucked her shaking hands under her arms. "Hello rats, are you up here?" Which was worse? Rodents scurrying around or the idea she'd let her aunt down?

Rats, she could scare. She stamped her feet, banged on the wall and paused. No sounds of rodents darting across the dusty wooden planks or rafters. Good. Near her sat three suitcases. She inhaled a cleansing breath, sat on a footstool and went to work listing each item and its condition.

Over an hour later, her cell phone rang from downstairs. She ran down the steps with her notebook in hand. Kevin's name popped up. At least her realtor wasn't outside with papers and pounding on her locked door. She grabbed her cell as it fell silent.

A loud bang shot out from the street. She flinched. *All right, stay calm. It was just a car backfiring.*

She crept to the front window. A man dressed in leathers exited the tattoo shop. The hour was growing late. She'd better get home. She could call Kevin later. After stowing away her notes, she shut off the lights. With umbrella in hand and her purse slung over her shoulder, she locked up the store. She turned to leave as a lime green sports car rolled up to the curb. Nash?

The window wound down, and he waved to her. "Hop in."

She settled into the passenger seat. "What brought you to my neighborhood?"

"You weren't home, and I wanted to see you."

His words sent a rush of pleasure mixed with guilt through her. She was breaking her no-more-men rule by falling for him. No use denying it. She shifted toward the side window. Out on the street, she spotted a navy sedan disappearing in the opposite direction. She turned in her seat, tracking the vehicle that slowed in front of her shop, and she caught the green and white New Hampshire plate.

Nash hung a right, cutting off her view.

"Something wrong?"

What would she say? A car slowed when it passed Now and Then? "Everything is fine."

"That's good. Now tell me what was in the package yesterday."

She debated for a moment, but gave in. "I used to receive his gifts in New York. They were lectures, sermons. Now I throw them away."

"Was it from Aaron?"

"Aaron doesn't have a post office where he is."

"His body was never recovered, and he emptied his bank account before he left. He has enough money to survive."

Ela threw him a surprised look.

"Sorry, I read up on him."

"You might as well know. He planned to use the money for us to run away, but he changed his mind when I wouldn't join him. I didn't disclose his intentions to anyone. I was embarrassed by the whole idea, plus we'd never have been able to return home." She dipped her head and let out a breath. "The coastguard spent days searching, without results. More than half a million people drown each year, approximately two people each minute." She recited the facts she'd learned and managed to keep the horror from her voice. *No regrets, no guilt.* "It's not uncommon for their bodies to disappear at sea. His parents spent a fortune, hiring ships to explore the waters near his boat. A friend of the Judge's, who owned a helicopter, flew over the area for a month."

"Do you accept that he died out there?"

She gripped the armrest. "I had a choice. Believe he's hiding somewhere, or he drowned. I considered the facts. The searchers found nothing except his boat with empty beer cans aboard, suggesting Aaron's judgment was impaired. He was a strong swimmer, but no one can survive for days in an open sea, and no sane person would have dared to go out during the storm to aid him in an escape scheme. The ocean was too dangerous that afternoon. No boats went out and others sailed to a harbor. Aaron either underestimated the storm or was caught in it.

"I'm sorry for the pain he caused you, Ela."

She wet her dry lips and felt the tightness in her chest. "My imagination conjures up scenes of him spotting searchers who didn't see or hear him and the terror he felt when they turned around." She saw him in the water. His hope disappearing as the rescue boat grew smaller and smaller in the vast sea. The scenario sent cold quivers up her spine. "Then I hope he hit his head when he fell overboard and never regained consciousness." She sighed. "I should have saved him."

"How? By commanding a vessel on the open sea? Were you in the coastguard?"

"I should have rented a boat, gone out and hunted for him. Instead, I stayed at home safe and dry and sat around while others searched."

"You've booked yourself a guilt trip. Jump off before you crash."

Anger spiked in her chest. He was like the rest, giving advice without understanding the facts.

He pulled into her driveway. "Tyler's car isn't here."

"He and Suz went out. Thanks for the ride."

He flashed that special smile, and she felt her resentment lower a degree, but not far enough. "You don't need to walk me to my door."

"I need to make sure you're safe before I leave."

He sounded kindhearted now, but he hadn't sounded that way when he talked about Aaron. "Why did you come again?"

He traced the curve of her chin with an unexpected gentleness. "I wanted to see you."

"You mentioned that earlier." She sat still, unsure what else to say and blotting out the sensation of his touch. The questioning light in his eyes suggested he was expecting a sign from her. *Now, tell him thanks, but no thanks.*

"I'm glad you came." No, that was wrong. She should have said, "Glad for the ride."

His smile of happiness touched her heart. "I'll walk you inside."

She slid out. Maybe she should make an excuse and send him away. Lock him out. She did neither. She strode along beside him, hoping for more.

Stop. Don't lead him on.

When she reached the door, she felt stronger. She focused on a spot over his shoulder. "Thanks for coming by." She spun around with her key in hand.

"I can stay for a while."

Just say no. The key turned. She opened the door. The world exploded with a flash of light.

CHAPTER 13

Nash raised his head. Ela lay a few feet from him on the ground. Ringing filled his ears. The scent of smoke warned him to move fast. He pushed to his feet. On unsteady legs, he swayed across the grass. "Ela!"

He crouched down next to her. Sweat soaked him. "Answer me, Ela."

Her eyelids fluttered open. She stared up with her gaze clouded. "What happened?"

"Something exploded in your house. Thank you, God, we're both alive."

"Excuse me, are you hurt?" asked a high-pitched voice.

Nash shifted his attention to a gray-haired lady who resembled an elderly elf. She stood on the edge of the lawn, wringing her hands. It was his mother's friend and Ela's neighbor.

"I heard the noise," she said, "and saw you both on the grass."

"Call nine-one-one," Nash told her.

The woman hurried away. Ela stirred.

"Don't move. The EMTs will come once she calls."

"I'm okay." She shoved strands of hair out of her smudged face.

"You shouldn't get up until you're checked out."

"I want to see what happened." With his support, she braced herself on her forearms and sat up. She swept a probing gaze over the yard and the front of the house, where smoke drifted from the opening. "Is that my door on the grass?"

128

"I guess you needed four locks."

"I'm glad your humor is still intact." She tilted her head back and sniffed. "Something's burning." She wrinkled her nose. "Call the fire department."

"Nine-one-one will contact them." He lowered her to the ground and searched for signs of a bruise or blood on her ash-white face. "Feel any pain?"

"I think I hit my head."

The sound of sirens announced the first emergency vehicle's arrival. A fire truck followed by an ambulance turned into the drive. Two middle-aged men and a plump, young woman leaped out of the ambulance and hustled over to Ela. On their blue overalls, they wore patches identifying them as Rockypoint EMTs.

"Help has arrived," Nash said as he held her cold hand. "I'll speak to the firefighters and be right back. Promise."

He left her surrounded by the three techs.

In the driveway, suited up firefighters jumped out of the truck and grabbed their gear. A stocky firefighter with a receding hairline approached Nash. "Do you live here?"

"I'm Nash McCain, a friend of Miss Danforth, the owner." He gestured to Ela who was having her blood pressure taken. "We were on the porch when a blast knocked out the front door and sent us flying to the lawn. We'd no warning. The neighbor called it in." He rubbed the back of his neck. Had he missed the odor of gasoline or propane? "Is there a fire inside? There's a lot of smoke pouring out of the house."

"We'll contain the blaze. It'll take a while before we can determine the cause of the flames. We inspect the entire building first."

Nash returned to Ela with the EMTs and squatted beside her.

"The explosion wrecked my hall table." She pointed at the gate-leg table now in two pieces a few feet away. Fragments from the Chinese vase lay scattered nearby. "What happened?"

"We won't know until they've completed their investigation. The smoke's disappeared already. The fire must have been in a small area inside the house."

A young medic in his twenties with short, brown hair informed Ela they were bringing the stretcher. He turned to

Nash. "The lady insists we take your vitals, too. Step over to the truck."

Ela caught his eye and mouthed, "Go."

He walked to the ambulance, where he sat in the front seat and answered the simple questions about the day of the week, the name of the president. After he was declared fit, he hopped out.

A cruiser pulled into the driveway, and the two patrol officers from the last call to the house emerged.

"Nash!" Tyler's compact car sped up the street with Suz leaning out an open window, yelling to him. The compact rolled up to the curb, and Suz was out before the engine died. On her crutches, she made her way across the yard toward the EMTs lifting Ela onto the stretcher.

"Stay out of the way, ma'am." The patrolman blocked Suz's path.

"That's my sister."

Nash scrambled to her side. "She's okay, Suz. Don't worry."

Suz spoke to the firefighters recoiling the hose outside the house. "We had a fire?" Her face crumpled. "Did I forget to turn off the toaster oven?"

Nash laid a hand on her arm. "The police and emergency personnel are looking into it. You should go with Ela in the ambulance. I'll follow."

"Why's she going if she's fine?"

"The medics are taking precautions. Hurry and catch up to them."

"I'll tell Tyler."

"I'll do it. Go." He spotted Tyler, who was shouting, "Wow!" by the porch.

One of the patrolmen approached Nash with a notepad and pen in his hand. "McCain, we met the other night. What happened today?"

Nash repeated the facts and the man scribbled away.

"I'm guessing you'd have been in worse shape if the door hadn't shielded you both," the officer said.

If the blast had gone off after Ela stepped inside, she'd be in pieces now. Near the drive, the EMTs finished loading her into the ambulance. He turned back to the policeman. "I'm done here. I'm following Ela to the hospital."

"You can't leave yet. I need to ask a few more questions for my report. "Stop," the officer shouted when Nash continued marching away to his vehicle.

"Later," Nash tossed over his shoulder. No one would prevent him from going with Ela. The transport was already pulling out on the road.

"Tyler, want to ride with me?" he called to the teen across the lawn. Nash jogged to his car and started the engine. Tyler jumped into the passenger seat. As they zipped away from the house, the Channel 23 News van parked at the curb. At least they'd escaped the press.

"Cool." Tyler's voice rose with excitement, and he ran his palm over the dashboard.

"First time?" Nash asked.

"Don't let Suz know, but yeah, I've never ridden in a sports car before. What happened at the house?"

"Explosion."

"Good thing Suz was with me. Usually I drop her off after school before I go to work. If I had, she would have been lying on the ground like a piece of litter. What blew?"

"I don't know." In the commotion afterwards, he'd functioned on autopilot. Now his adrenaline dropped a degree, and his brain cleared to consider if whatever discharged was accidental or set by their stalker.

Was it meant for Suz and a coincidence that the explosion happened when Ela arrived, or was someone stalking her and aware of her movements? "Suz is typically the first one home?"

"Yeah, Ela rolls in around five thirty except nights the library is open late and she works. You think the guy who forced Suz off Dead Man's Curve bombed their home?" Tyler's eyes widened. "He didn't get her on the curve so he's trying again?"

Nash shook his head at Tyler. "Before, you were convinced the driver was a kid attempting to break a speed record. Are you changing your mind now and saying someone meant to knock Suz off the road?"

Tyler shrugged. "All the kids race each other up the hill, but I can't think of anyone trying to break a record for setting off explosives in people's homes."

"You and me both, Tyler. Did you give the police the kids' names?"

"The cops already talked to them at school. Nobody had it in for Suz. They're into cars and racing."

At the hospital, they entered a waiting room with box couches and matching chairs lined against the beige wall. No one else was inside. A desk and computer stood behind a glassed-in counter with a sign instructing them to sit until called. A nurse in a flowered smock took their information and directed them to the empty seats.

"Since it's a slow day in emergency, the doctors should tend to Ela without delays," Nash told Tyler.

"Tyler!" Suz appeared. She swung across the room on her crutches and into his arms. After a second, she broke free and spoke to Nash. "The nurse wouldn't let me stay with Ela."

"We'll hear soon." Nash ushered them to the chairs, but he decided pacing made the minutes pass faster. His thoughts skipped from his first meeting with Ela at the hospital, where she'd looked vulnerable, yet tough, to today and back again.

Tyler plopped into a seat beside Suz who recited a series of possible causes for the explosion from leaving the toaster oven on to someone tossing a firecracker at the house.

Finally, she rose and approached Nash, who was walking the perimeter of the industrial style carpet. "Tyler and I are going to scout out the cafeteria for the pizza competition. Tyler thinks they carry a frozen brand. Bored enough to come?"

"I'll stay. We should hear something any minute."

Once they left, Nash went out on the sidewalk and called his dad, explaining the situation. He clicked off his phone as Ballard strode up the walkway from the parking lot.

"Can't keep out of trouble, can you, McCain. Where's Lanie?"

"She's safe with her grandmother."

"Why don't you go home to your daughter?"

"I'm here for Ela Danforth."

"Is she your girlfriend or your client?"

"She's my friend and client. What's your problem, Ballard? Cindy's been gone for almost three years. You act like she died yesterday and I personally had a hand in her death. If you visited your niece, you'd remember we're family."

"I won't forget what you did to my sister." He drew closer, his voice low and menacing. The muscles in his arms bulged under the sleeves of his uniform.

"I'm guilty of loving her. Nothing else," Nash ground out between clenched teeth.

"Where were you when Lanie was born? Where were you all those nights when Cindy took care of her? You should have been with your wife and daughter instead of at law school or with your books in the library. You could have taken those classes anytime. My sister was always alone in her marriage."

Ballard's closeness and words tempted Nash to swing at him. Instead, he did his best to keep his voice under control. "When you cut back on your work hours, talk to me."

"I don't have a child and wife who need me. You were never there for yours, McCain. Everyone knew what caused my sister's problems."

"I wasn't perfect, but I cared for Cindy, and Lanie was born to both of us, not just her mother."

His last statement seemed to snap Ballard out of their tug of words. He stepped back from Nash. "I'm here to speak with Miss Danforth on police business."

"I'll find out from the desk clerk how much longer until Ela can see us. Don't forget. I'm her lawyer. I'll be present when you ask her questions."

The men stomped inside, keeping a measured distance between them. The nurse brought them into another room five minutes later. Ela lay in a raised hospital bed, separated from others by curtains. Bruises were already forming on her forehead and around her eyes.

"Nash?" She pushed herself further up against the pillow. "Can I leave now?"

"Chief Ballard wants to ask you a few questions. You don't have to answer them if you're not up to it."

"I'm ready." She focused on the detective at the foot of the bed. "Someone is trying to hurt my sister, and I believe her crash on the hill wasn't an accident. I hope you'll arrest whoever is responsible soon."

"Sorry, Miss Danforth," Ballard said. "We're still

investigating. Looks like whoever set up the explosive in your house used a rear window for entrance." Ballard took out his notebook and pen. "We're expanding our inquiry. You should be able to name a person or two who carried a grudge toward your sister or yourself. We both know about your father's problems. Given the hill's history of accidents, I didn't believe his crimes were responsible for Suz's, but now, with your additional troubles, I've added another theory and possible suspects."

Nash touched her shoulder. "Do you want to rest?"

She shook her head. "You've given up the idea a local is harassing us?"

"No, I'm just throwing the net wider," Ballard said. "We'll be looking at your former clients. After their losses, they might track down a family member for revenge."

"You're right," Ela said. "Plenty of people would love for us to fall off the earth. If you need a list, request one from the United States Attorney's office of New York City."

"Got it." Ballard's tightened his lips. "Go over what occurred at your house an hour ago."

She recited the facts in a steady voice. When she reached the end, Ballard snapped his notes closed.

"We'll expect a copy of the report on the explosion," Nash said.

"We'll be in touch, McCain, and I'll be speaking with the DA in New York. I'm finished for the time being." The detective crossed the floor and left.

"Ballard never seems like he's on my side." She sank back into her pillow. Her bruises stood out against the white sheets.

"I'm on your side."

"That's all I need." She reached up and wove her fingers through his, and just like that he felt her open her heart to him.

CHAPTER 14

Two hours later, Ela waited for the doctor's okay to go home. She replayed for the hundredth time walking from Nash's car to the door before the explosion, and then, twining their fingers together in the hospital.

"Excuse me."

She looked up to find a man with a white collar near her bed curtain. He was Nash's pastor, the one she'd met at the hospital when she'd visited Suz.

"I heard about your accident and came to see if you needed anything."

"Thank you, no." She glanced away, hoping he'd leave without a discussion.

"I won't interrupt your rest."

He'd begun toward the door when the old doubt popped into her mind. "Pastor, just a minute. I've a problem that's been bothering me."

He paused. "I'll try to answer unless it's for your doctor."

"My question is for you, in a way."

"I'm listening." He took a couple of steps closer to her bed with his white brows furrowed.

Ideas bounced in her head while she tried to decide how much to reveal. She'd let the thoughts flow out of her mouth. "Someone's leading a good life, and then one day, everything goes wrong and you're treated like you slaughter little children for fun. How can a person believe in the goodness of others when they turn their backs when you need them most?"

The pastor's intense gaze and silence made her uneasy. She

135

bent her head and smoothed the blanket. Why had she brought up the subject?

"Sometimes we lose our way and have to search more than others, but once we're on the right path, you find people who will reach out to help. Then we reciprocate by paying it forward in good deeds or actions."

Did he mean New York had been the wrong path and that was why everything had fallen apart, or was New York a metaphor for the way she'd led her life? When was the last time she'd extended a hand or offered her friendship to another?

Footsteps sounded on the other side of the curtain, and Nash emerged with a smile until his gaze landed on Pastor Smith. Nash blinked and stopped.

"Thanks for stopping by, Pastor," Ela rushed to say, and slid a glance at Nash.

The reverend said hello to Nash as he left.

"Everything okay?" he asked Ela, and approached the bed.

"Don't worry. I wasn't receiving the last rites. He was visiting the ill. It's part of his job, and we had an interesting conversation."

"I'm glad."

She lifted her chin and twisted the cuff of the blanket, unsure how far she wanted to carry the topic. Ending it seemed the best. "I told the doctor I'm ready to go home. I need to fix my house and put in a big alarm system."

"They're still investigating at your place. Let me offer my guest bedroom to you and Suz. Lanie will be thrilled, and I hope Suz won't mind her new fan's attention."

"I don't want to intrude."

"You won't. My father showed up a few minutes ago with Lanie, and we exchanged vehicles. I have plenty of room to drive everyone to my house. Suz and Lanie are in the waiting room, and Tyler was called into work to replace a sick employee. My dad gave him a ride to his car."

Nash had thought of everything. "Thanks. We'd love to join you and Lanie for the evening."

"You're welcome. I'll talk to the nurse and find out when you can leave." He disappeared from the room.

Ela lay on the bed and let the idea sink in. She was going to

Nash's home. Would she find reminders of his wife? She died three years ago, yet people kept remembrances. Look at Aunt Vickie's house. Though comparing someone to her aunt who loved the past was not fair. But how much did Nash love his past?

He returned with a nurse in tow, and the discharge formalities were completed. In the parking lot, he assisted Ela into the front of his father's SUV. Lanie and Suz settled in the rear.

"Next stop, the McCain residence." He keyed the engine.

Ela's thoughts drifted to Nash. He'd been her rock throughout the evening and now she was falling deeper into his debt and his invisible web of attraction. She could drift away on this new wave of happiness. She studied him. His whiskered jaw was strong—maybe a little too strong and angular. His hazel eyes could glitter with humor or fierceness, depending on the conversation, and those large, steady hands... Mentally, she sighed. Most of all, he was willing to help her, but people who helped could get hurt or worse. Her elation spiraled downward. How selfish was she to entangle him in her problems?

"This is temporary," she blurted. "I don't want to drag you into my mess. We're going home tomorrow."

"Did you hear me protesting?" He sent her his dazzling smile.

"You won't charm me into changing my mind, Nash."

"Do it for Suz, then."

Ela shook her head. "Sometimes, you read me too easily." She'd give in for now, but the arrangement ended in the morning.

During the ride, Lanie chatted about her home and described each room. By the time they arrived in the driveway of the saltbox style home, Ela could have gone inside and walked to Lanie's room based on the young girl's description.

Lanie jumped out first, and yelled for Suz to beat her to the house. Nash opened Ela's door and took her elbow to guide her. Her curiosity was running high, and she found herself as eager as the girls for the tour of Nash's home.

"Watch your step. Do you have any dizziness?" He held onto her arm.

"No vertigo." She smiled to hide the truth. She was suffering a few aches, but more distracting was her reaction to his touch.

Lanie was jumping up and down on the front steps. "Hurry, Dad. I want to show Ela the house. Suz already saw it."

"Ela needs to rest."

"I'd love to see your room. You won't be playing baseball in it, will you?" Ela teased, and moved away from Nash while he dug out his key.

Lanie lowered her head and peeked up at her father. "I'm not allowed to toss the ball inside, but we've a big yard with a fence if Suz wants me to throw to her."

"The McCain ball field closed at dark, Lanie," Nash's stern voice reminded her.

"All right. We never have company except my grandparents and Suz. Lanie hopped from foot to foot while Nash inserted the key.

"Should I stand near the car while you open up?" Ela teased, yet she winced when the lock clicked.

Lanie shot inside and ran back to encourage them to move faster.

"Why don't you get a plate of cookies and give our visitors a few minutes to settle in?"

"Suz, Ela, do you want milk, too?" Lanie asked.

"Ela drinks a lot of tea," Suz said. "I'll help you make it."

The girls disappeared together, leaving Ela with Nash alone in the tiled entryway. Did she look poised and calm instead of how she really felt, nervous and self-conscious?

"I'll show you the guestroom before our hostess returns."

Upstairs was his room and Cindy's. Eagerly, she followed him upward and let her curiosity override her other emotions.

"If you feel ill, we can stop. Lanie's keyed up since you're her first official guest. By the time I pick her up from her grandparents, I'm ready for supper, the dishes, homework and sleep. I save a couple of weekends a month for father and daughter occasions."

"Sounds like a full life." Without room for anyone else.

They climbed toward what must be the bedrooms. She lifted her head, straining to catch sight of his room.

He brought her to the second door in the hallway. "You have your own bathroom," he said, pausing for her to enter.

The room was blue walls with beige molding. An ivory quilt

covered a queen size bed, and a tall chest of drawers stood against the opposite wall. "It's big."

"Originally, it was the master and the one room Cindy decorated. It took her a year to decide on color and furniture, and then, we didn't move in." He tugged the curtains closed over the double windows. "No one will be spying on you tonight."

A strong surge of relief set free the attraction that hummed in her body. She tried to ignore it by studying the room and searching for signs of Cindy's personal touch. Simple but elegant described the bedroom and probably the woman.

"When did you buy this house?"

"We bought it the year before Cindy died. I thought a new place would cheer her up. I underestimated her problem. A walk-in is over here." He motioned to the closet, and Ela sensed he needed to change the topic. "I hope Suz doesn't mind sharing the guest room with you."

"She wouldn't be my sister if she didn't complain, but if you put her in a strange bedroom by herself, she'd sneak into mine. Nash, I appreciate all you've done for me and Suz." She twisted Aunt Vickie's sapphire ring on her finger as her ever-stronger feelings for him bubbled upward.

He stood less than a foot from her. She spotted new whiskers darkening his chin. She moistened her lips and hurried to fill the silence between them. "You've gone out of your way for us, and I owe you so much."

"You're the one who's had the tough day. Anything else you need?"

Back away. Say good night. You just left the hospital. She shut out the annoying voice in her head and rose up on her toes to thank him.

She grazed his lips before the knock on the door interrupted them. She jumped back with her heart leaping out of her chest, the sensation of the pressure of his mouth against hers.

Suz walked in holding a tray of cookies and a mug. "Surprise. I brought your snack." She hesitated. "Something wrong?"

Did she look guilty? "I didn't expect you to serve me. That's all." She clasped her hands together and smiled at Suz.

"Is Lanie still in the kitchen?" Nash asked.

He was standing a yard away from her. How did he get that far?

"She's choosing a special mug for you."

"I'd better go downstairs and help her. Excuse me." He walked toward the hall and stopped. "I stored some of Cindy's clothes in a trunk in the closet. Help yourself."

Now she could wear his deceased wife's outfits in their former master bedroom. Talk about a romance killer. "I'm good, Nash," she told him before he shut the door.

Suz laid the tray on the bureau and grabbed a cookie. "Ballard talked to me outside the hospital. He wanted to know if I'd thought of anyone yet who'd hurt me either here or New York. He still would love to pin it on Tyler, my one friend."

Pain for her sister stabbed Ela. "I'm sorry, Suz. Starting over in Rockypoint seemed a good idea when we inherited the house. Now it's like we tried to run away from our problems, and they chased us." She sank onto the edge of the mattress.

"I'm not sorry." Suz's face brightened. "I wouldn't have met Tyler if we stayed in New York. You wouldn't have met Nash." She wriggled her eyebrows.

"Don't plan a double wedding."

"El, Aaron disappeared over a year ago." Suz rested her cookie on the tray.

"I thought you missed him."

"Can't I like Nash, too? Isn't that okay?"

"Of course, Suz. Our hearts are big enough for millions of people."

"When we were in New York, you and Aaron were an awesome couple, but you're different in Rockypoint." She gawked at Ela as if she'd grown another face.

Ela shrugged. "Yes, I've changed. I once worked in a well-respected Manhattan financial office. Now I push a little cart around and shelve books. I live in a house that's over a hundred years old and full of what a lot of people call junk, but some call antiques. And my sister lives with me. For therapy, I cook or shop from the TV or a website. If Aaron were alive today, he wouldn't recognize me."

"Do you hate your life?"

"No, Suz. I'm the fortunate one." Aaron wasn't.

The flash of a memory lit her mind like a streak of lightening. "The police are going to arrest me." Aaron's tense voice had told her he was fighting for control. "They think I'm part of your father's schemes."

"You're innocent." She slapped her palm against her black-skirted knee. "The DA should consider my father was too greedy or worried about getting caught to share his illegal gains."

Aaron shoved his shaking hands into the pockets of his suit coat. "I've hired a lawyer, but he costs both my arms, legs and future grandchildren. By the time he's done, I won't be able to afford a pencil. This will kill my family. I'm losing everything."

"You still have me," she said, desperate to end his pain.

The expression on his face changed from sad to cynical. "You're worth my entire life?"

His answer hit her directly in the heart and left her breathless and confused. "What—did you say?"

"Ela." Suz waved her hand in front of her sister's face.

Ela dragged her thoughts back to the present. "What, Suz?"

Suz stood at the window, peeking out between the floor length curtains. "If I were Nash, I wouldn't let us in his house. This crazy person could rig another bomb, a bigger one, and blow up Nash and Lanie with us."

Ela forced the nagging alarm ringing in her head into silence. "The bomber is busy hiding from Ballard and his men. We're safe." She wouldn't voice her own fears and scare Suz.

"If it's the guy from SOC, why would he want to hurt me?" Suz asked. "I don't even know him."

"He's ill, but the police will find him." Ela crossed the floor to Suz at the window and stared out into the clear night. A full moon hung in the sky, but dark clouds surrounded it, threatening to smother its light. She put an arm around her sister and waited for her to shrug it off. Instead, her sister's warm body melted against hers and brought back memories of the little sister from only a few months ago. Ela was certain about one thing. She'd do anything to protect Suz.

Lanie appeared to continue her hostess services after Ela sipped her tea and ate a snack from the plate.

The young girl toured them around her purple bedroom, and then she and Suz disappeared into the garage, where Lanie wanted to show off the birdhouses she and her grandfather had built for the nearby marsh.

Ela wandered into the large kitchen with granite counter tops and stainless steel appliances. In the dining nook sat a card table with metal chairs. On the other side of the room, a patio door was ajar.

She crossed to the open glass slider. A cool, damp breeze flowed through and reminded her of the awakening spring. She peeked out on to the porch, where the kitchen light spilled onto the planked floor of the screened-in space.

"You escaped? I heard voices in the garage."

Ela hesitated a second for her eyes to adjust to the dim figure of Nash sitting on a wooden glider in the shadows. Their brief kiss was still on her mind.

"Lanie's showing off her birdhouses. Are you up for company?"

He patted the seat next to him. "Come and join me."

Together on the back porch with Nash. Who'd have thought such a simple request would be the most tempting invitation she'd had in a long time? Why not pretend for a few moments she had a normal life and a man who cared about her? "Let me grab my jacket."

She put on her coat in the hallway and returned to the porch. She eased into the spot beside him, aware of his thigh pressing against her leg on the two-seater. Nerves jumped in her stomach, and she stared out into the blackness over the yard, while conscious of each breath Nash drew.

"You don't need a kitchen table?" she asked, trying for small talk.

"The fold up table was temporary, but I never got around to changing it. We eat out a lot, or at my parents' house."

"No wonder the appliances look brand new." The sound of peepers croaking carried across the yard. "Not much traffic passes on your road."

Girls' laughter escaped through the shared wall of the attached garage.

"I guess it's not too quiet." Her gaze roamed over the back lawn, and a new awareness ended her sense of security. "Do you think he's out there watching us?"

"You're safe, Ela."

The certainty in his voice gave her confidence. She nodded,

and his features became more distinct in the dimness. She stared at his profile. "You must love the peacefulness."

"The builder spaced the houses for privacy, yet you're not alone. In the summer, there are hundreds of fireflies in the yard. Lanie loves to catch them. Of course, she releases them."

"Where did you live before you bought this house?"

"We owned a smaller, older home closer to my parents. Cindy picked this one out. She talked a lot about how she wanted decorate it, but she never finished. I'm sure you noted the lawn furniture in the formal living room. We never got around to picking out a set. Lanie and I don't sit in there much. We're in the TV room most of the time."

"Lanie must miss her mother."

"She asks a lot of questions." He shifted toward Ela. "I can't answer some of them. What was her mom's favorite food? For a long time, I blotted out the personal memories that caused me pain. Do you know Aaron's favorite food?"

"I do because he brought me to his favorite Italian restaurant near the office every week."

"Cindy and I were in love when we married, and I'm positive she could answer all those questions about me. After Lanie was born, the doctor diagnosed Cindy with postpartum depression. We both believed she'd get better." He shook his head. "Her mental health deteriorated, and our lives changed forever. Every day was a challenge for her. What I remember most is the effort it took her to get up and dressed. I thought she was just tired." His voice became husky. "I've blamed myself for leaving her alone too much." He pushed the glider back and forth. The motion comforted her, eased away the stresses of the day, but she felt the tenseness in his leg pressed to hers.

"Absence can't cause a disease."

"I'm sure it didn't help. I thought it was temporary, but the depression deepened even when I was home and Lanie grew older. Ballard's not completely right or wrong."

"Aaron felt his life was ruined because of me and my father."

"That's ridiculous."

"His parents and brother seemed to agree at his memorial. They were cool toward Suz and me."

"Don't own their problems."

"Are you offering personal advice, McCain?"

"It sounds like we're a pair."

A pair? Silence stretched between them. The day had been awful and full of threats, but now a new risk surfaced while she sat in the dark with Nashua McCain. She felt his hip snug against hers. Warmth from his body seeped into her. What would it be like to end every day sitting on the porch glider with this man?

"I bet Lanie's digging out my old baseball gear in the garage. She's been fascinated with the sport since she and Suz tossed around my ball."

His words broke the drift of her thoughts. "They haven't shattered a window tonight."

"Disasters averted, so far. I'm glad Lanie's interested. I told her we'd practice catch in the backyard, but I haven't found time yet."

"When we moved to New Hampshire, I hoped Suz would find interests. She used to love ballet, but she stopped lessons after Dad was arrested."

His fingers brushed the nape of her neck as he settled his arm around the back of the swing, and she had to force herself to focus on his words.

"Was Suz ready to leave the Big Apple?"

"She was. Her social life wasn't going well, and for a teenager what else is there?" Ela raised one shoulder slightly. "We never had the funds for her ballet again."

"I'm glad you're in Rockypoint. I take it as a sign."

"A sign of what?"

"That it's okay to kiss you."

She stopped breathing, and anticipation held her still. His fingers slid around her shoulder. Heat from his palm soaked into her jacket. She was aware of his every move toward her and the realization that now would be the time to say goodnight. But she didn't move.

Her heart pounded and the light in his eyes made her breath catch. His warm mouth came down over hers and all her doubts floated away, one by one. She leaned toward his broad chest, and a jolt of happiness rocked through her.

"Dad! Dad! Where are you?"

Nash released her and sat back in the swing. "We're on the porch."

The sound of scurrying footsteps dashed toward them. "There you are." Lanie popped into the doorway. "Suz went to bed."

"Good idea. You should go to yours. You've school tomorrow. If you'll excuse us, Ela, I'll help my daughter get ready for tomorrow."

"I'm ready to go upstairs, too." Ela popped off the swing and felt it hit the back of her thighs. Time for her to go, too. At least her day had ended on a promise of more.

"I'll see you in the morning, Nash, Lanie." She headed for the stairs and overheard Nash quizzing Lanie about completing her nighttime routine. Ela tiptoed into the guest bedroom. Suz lay in the double bed with the comforter tucked under her chin.

"Sorry," Suz said without moving. "I was so tired I came upstairs."

"Shush, go to sleep." A night light burned next to the bureau, but darkness fell over most of the room. The temptation to rejoin Nash crept over her. He was only a short distance away. It would be easy to stay until Lanie went to bed and then slip from the room and go to him....

CHAPTER 15

At midnight, Nash abandoned attempts at sleep, dressed and grabbed his laptop from the hallway table. A soft light shone under the guestroom door. He slowed and debated knocking on it. No, Ela would let him know if she needed anything.

He tramped onward, allowing the path of nightlights to guide him downstairs. After Lanie's mother died, he'd plugged them in for her. Each night she'd wake over and over with nightmares. He never learned what happened in her dreams. Only light and his presence had soothed her enough to fall asleep.

In the kitchen, he sat at the card table and opened the PC. Once the machine booted up, he typed in the URL for findaaronwright. He scrolled through the brief bio he'd written at the top of the page, past the image of the lit memorial candle and down to the comment section. Two people had left remarks in the remembrance box. The first wrote about a life lost too soon.

Nash read the next one. "Aaron was an honest young man who the world misjudged. He died before the truth was told. The person responsible for his downfall was never punished."

Both senders used a common webmail address that provided no clues as to their locations, and he might be on a false trail. The posters might know nothing about Aaron's true demise or left messages to lead him off track. Nash stretched his arms and caught sight of a glow outside. He went still. A beam shone on the edge of his property bounded by the chain link fence. Beyond were the woods managed by the Rockypoint Conservation Committee. The shaft of light traveled forward, parallel to his yard, and then disappeared.

A chill settled in his gut. He shut the top of his laptop and sidled to the patio door. The lock was flimsy, but the metal rod in the door's track secured the glass slider. He peered out and searched for what must be a person with a flashlight.

In the distance, the howl of a dog carried to the house. Was the person in the woods a neighbor in search of a pet, or someone spying? He removed the rod and stepped into the darkness of the porch. A whistle and the sound of something bounding through the brush floated in the chilly air.

The dog fell silent. The shaft of light moved away from his house and disappeared. Several seconds ticked past without a glimmer or a bark.

He secured the door before he retreated to his bedroom and removed the gun from the locked desk drawer in the alcove. With weapon in hand, he strode though the silent house and examined the bolt for each door and window. He returned to the kitchen where he stood by the window over the sink and angled his head for a view of the evening sky.

The stars shone, and a three-quarter moon hung in the blackness. He moved away and gazed at the spot where he'd last seen the light. Had the person been standing there long before calling his dog, staring at Nash's home? No one was around now.

Tomorrow he'd speak to Ela about home security and put more precautions in place. He would make sure everyone in his care was protected.

The next morning, Nash discovered Ela in an oversized robe, retrieving clothes from the dryer in the laundry room off the kitchen. "Did you get up in the middle of the night to wash clothes?"

She shot upward, wide-eyed with her mouth open. Her features smoothed into a smile. "Nash, I didn't hear you. I couldn't sleep. So I got up and fixed some tea, and since Suz would rather face another bomb than show up in the same clothes at school, I did laundry. I told her she could stay home, but she insisted she was going to her classes. I guess I'm a slow learner when it comes to reverse psychology."

"There's no predicting a teen, I guess. You must be feeling okay."

"I am." Ela tugged out the gray blouse she'd worn yesterday. "We're switching outfits, though Suz doesn't care for my black pants and button down shirt. She says I dress like a mortician."

"Life is demanding in high school."

"I, on the other hand, am excited to wear jeans and a t-shirt to shelve books. Want me to cook breakfast for you and Lanie? Suz, of course, avoids starting her day with healthy nourishment."

"Thanks, but Lanie always eats instant oatmeal, and I buy a muffin and coffee from the stand near my office. I do my part to support the locals. Help yourself to the oatmeal. Not much is in the fridge, I'm afraid."

"I'd love oatmeal. If you'll excuse me, I'll get dressed first." She folded the clothes over her arm and brushed past him. The scent of clean clothes trailed after her.

He raised his voice. "I've one more question."

She paused three feet from him, looking vulnerable in the giant robe.

"When you were up during the night, did you notice anything unusual?"

She shook her head. "Sorry, can you give me a hint?"

"I did some late work on my laptop and thought I saw a flashlight on the edge of the woods. Whoever it was disappeared after a minute and seemed to be calling a dog. "I didn't see lights or an animal. Should I worry?" She hugged Suz's t-shirt against her chest, and the crinkle appeared on her forehead.

"It was probably someone looking for his pet. The animal must have gotten away and led its owner on a chase."

Her shoulders lowered, and she expelled a breath. "Now that my morning is off to a creepy start, I'm going upstairs."

He closed the space between them. "Ela, I didn't mean to scare you, but we need to be on guard. You and Suz should stay here, where you're safe and not alone."

"I appreciate your concern. In fact...." She leaned toward him and kissed his mouth.

His hand went around the curve of her waist. The fuzzy robe was soft against his palm. Her lips tasted of cinnamon tea.

"Dad! Can we go to the mall?" Lanie called from the stairs.

He struggled with the urge to ignore his daughter and then

released Ela. "I should answer or she'll keep yelling."

"I need to get dressed." A blush rose in her cheeks. "Thanks for sharing your home."

"Dad!" Lanie appeared in the hall. "Can we go to the mall after school today and buy my school supplies?"

"Sounds like a plan."

"You can talk about your shopping while I get ready." Ela disappeared from the room.

An hour later, everyone packed into his father's car, ready for their day. Nash delivered Lanie to her school and then insisted on waiting while Ela clued Suz's principal in on their situation.

When Ela finished, Nash drove to her house. The yellow police tape surrounding the property's perimeter fluttered in the breeze, and the brown Major Crime van sat in the driveway. Police vehicles lined the street.

"They must be inside. You can let me off any place. I'll be safe."

"I'm not letting you off. We'll walk in together."

"Don't you have to go to your office?"

"I've an in with the boss." He parked on the next block, and they headed toward the Victorian.

"I checked my phone earlier," she said, keeping her gaze focused ahead. "Several people from the library left text messages after last night's explosion. They were shocked, and asked if they could help Suz and me."

"And you told them no."

She waved her hand about in the air. "There's nothing to do. Chief Ballard is on the porch. I want to speak to him." She broke into a trot before Nash could answer.

He joined Ela and Ballard near the missing front door. The opening was now covered by a blue tarp. The Chief flicked a glance at Nash but otherwise paid him no notice.

Ela turned to Nash. "Chief Ballard was informing me my bomber was an amateur who used a short fuse, which caused the explosive to probably go off earlier than he planned."

"Does that mean he was in the house or nearby when the device detonated?" Something about the timeline wasn't right.

"I'd estimate he lit it minutes before you arrived," Ballard announced, staring over Nash's head.

"I've noticed a navy sedan hanging around lately," Ela interjected. "I didn't see who was inside, but the car was a four-door and has New Hampshire plates. Sorry, I didn't catch the number. I've been too focused on trying to figure out if the driver's following me or just happens to be going my way."

"You didn't mention this to me before?" Ballard's eyebrows shot upward.

"There was always a logical reason for the car."

"Ela, I wish you'd told me, but I can guarantee whoever was on Moose Hill wasn't in a sedan," Nash said. "We're either dealing with more than one person or an individual with more than one vehicle." As soon as the words left his mouth, his thoughts turned to Tyler, who could access different forms of transportation from his father's garage.

"My men are canvassing the neighborhood," Ballard said. "I'll find out if anyone's spotted the sedan." He glanced at his watch. "I've a noon meeting at the station. We should be done here by then." He marched away.

"We need to take bigger precautions," Nash insisted when Ballard was out of earshot.

"We?" Ela raised her chin. "You don't have to take on more of my problems."

"Quit the tough act, Ela. Like it or not, I'm going to worry about you. Get used to the idea. It happens when people like each other."

"I appreciate your concern, but—"

"Too late to protest. I won't change my mind."

"Stubborn man." Her voice held a note of affection. "Since I'm not allowed inside for a while, how about a ride, and you can worry about me on the way?"

"Let's go."

When they arrived at the library, he walked Ela to her cart loaded with books.

"Guess I'll be busy." She ran a finger up the pile.

"Call if you hear anything from Ballard." He kissed her, and she blushed again. He was tempted to kiss her once more, but resisted the urge. He'd make up for it later.

* * *

Ela left work early when a co-worker offered her a ride home. The police had removed the yellow tape. She pushed aside the tarp and walked through the empty hall to the parlor.

Inside, a soggy chair, puddles of water and relocated furniture were signs left from the search and fire. Knickknacks were piled up on the parlor coffee table.

At least she could put everything back together before Suz arrived. Hopefully, the chair would dry and be okay or she'd snare another from the shop. First, she measured for the new exterior door.

Finished, she went to work straightening the bedrooms. Thirty minutes later, Suz still hadn't arrived. Ela took out her cell from her purse and pushed the numbers for her sister. Of course she'd ignore her call and later plead she was too busy to talk.

She counted the rings. "One...tw—"

"Ela! I'm at the police station."

"Suz? It's you."

"Who else would answer my phone? Never mind. The police think Tyler bombed our house. Two detectives asked him to come to the station when we walked to his car after school. Where's Nash? I can't reach him. He has to come. Tyler needs a lawyer."

"Calm down. Nash is at his office, as far as I know. Why do the police suspect Tyler of causing the blast?"

"I don't know. Tyler said he'd look guilty if he didn't go. They've kept him for almost an hour and won't let me see him. It's police brutality."

"Let me try calling Nash."

"Tell him his client needs help." She clicked off.

Ela punched in Nash's number, and the call went to his voicemail. At the beep, she left a message.

She pocketed her cell, shrugged on her jacket and started across the yard. Her neighbor was watching from her window. Ela waved and proceeded to the sidewalk. Twenty minutes later, she entered the police station.

Suz jumped up from a plastic chair against the white wall. "Tyler hasn't come out." She stared past Ela. "Where's Nash? In the parking lot?"

Ela unbuttoned her jacket. The room felt like it was ninety

degrees. They must sweat the truth from suspects. "I didn't get in touch with him."

"What? He has to come. He's Tyler's lawyer."

"Suz, Tyler can't afford Nash, and we can't expect him to drop his paying clients for us."

"Nash and I had an agreement. I sit for him and he represents Tyler."

Her sister was out of touch with reality. "You can't pretend that's an equal arrangement."

"He agreed to the deal, and I'm a reliable babysitter, if you forget about the broken lamp."

Ela shook her head and approached the uniformed clerk, who was studying them with open curiosity from behind the front desk.

"I'm Ela Danforth, and I need to speak to Chief Ballard."

"Is this about a crime?" the young, rail-thin woman asked.

"Yes it is. I've important information for him."

The clerk pushed a number on the desk phone and spoke in clipped words.

Suz seemed to bounce up and down with nervous energy.

The clerk hung up. "The chief can't see you at the moment. One of the other officers can take your statement."

"He's busy beating up my boyfriend," Suz yelled.

Ela winced. "I'm sure no one is beating anyone, including Chief Ballard."

"I'm not sure I'd take you up on the bet." Nash crossed the hall to the desk and directed his attention to the woman on the other side. "I'm Nashua McCain and Tyler Rawlings's legal counsel. I believe you've detained my client. You can take me to him now."

"You have to let him in. He's a lawyer." Suz fisted a hand on top of the counter.

"I don't need you telling me how to do my job, little girl. Mr. McCain, you'll have to wait a minute." The woman pressed another number on the desk phone and turned from them to speak.

Nash stepped away from the clerk and motioned for them to join him.

"You'll get Tyler out, right, Nash?" Suz said to him. "No

one's heard of 'innocent until proven guilty' in this place."

"Suz, calm down. You're not helping by insulting people." Ela put a hand on her sister's rigid shoulder.

"Sometimes we play nicer than we feel," Nash said in a low voice. "First, I'll get Tyler released."

"Mr. McCain, follow me." The clerk rose and waved a hand in the air.

Suz started forward.

"Not you." The clerk pointed at Suz. "Mr. McCain, this way."

Nash followed the woman through the metal detector and disappeared through a side door.

"Ela, Tyler and I are moving away."

"What are you talking about?" Ela faced Suz.

"You and I moved to Rockypoint to get a new start. Well, our new start blew up in your face, and my boyfriend is on the verge of going to jail. I can't stay in Rockypoint any longer, and Tyler is leaving with me."

"Suz, you can't decide a major life change when you're stressed. After we leave the station, we'll sit and discuss your options."

"Tyler and I talked over our choices and agreed to go. You can't chain me to my bed."

"Suz, you can't build your life around Tyler."

"Why not? You were building your life around Aaron. Mom built her life around Dad. She was happy until the last two years. If Tyler and I last as long as dad and mom, I'll be happy."

"What if you're together less than a month?"

"Then I'll be happy for a month. It sounds better to me than being escorted around like a prisoner and worrying the police will arrest Tyler."

"Suz, you could end up stranded, with no money or home. At least wait until the police catch the criminal who's threatening you."

"I'd have to wait years for the Rockypoint Police to arrest anyone, except for Tyler, and they want *him,* because they can't think of anybody else. I'm not you, Ela. I'll risk a chance with my boyfriend."

Suz's words brought up the question: what if she'd taken a chance and gone on Aaron's boat the day he disappeared?

"Let's run away, Ela." The remembrance of Aaron's last appeal yanked her into the past. "We'll get married and forget the craziness of trials, lawyers and plea bargains. We'll have a life someplace else. We'll sail off to an island to live. The Judge will help us. I'll talk to him."

"I can't leave my father. Besides, people will think we ran off because we were guilty."

"Ela! Are you daydreaming?"

She blinked, returned to the present with a thud and blurted out the first thing to enter her head. "Suz, you can't move out. I forbid it."

"I'm not your slave. Stop ordering me around. And I'm not perfect like you are. I guess I'm more like Dad. Maybe you'll pretend I don't exist, too."

Shock and guilt blocked Ela's throat. She couldn't speak.

Her sister's face hardened. "I'll hang outside for Tyler. Don't count on me coming home.

I'm done with Snoreville. I'm doing what I want and not what everyone else wants me to do." She stomped through the exit.

Ela became conscious of the clerk staring at her. She sank onto the hard chair. Maybe she and Suz should leave town together. They'd moved to Rockypoint to find peace, and they'd found none.

"Ela." Tyler waved to her as he and Nash walked through the metal detector and entered the lobby.

She ran across the floor to meet them. "Tyler, are you free to go?"

"Thanks to my lawyer." He hooked his thumb at Nash. "He's the best." Tyler swept a glance around the room. "Where's Suz?"

"She's outside."

He started toward the door.

"Tyler," Nash said. "Soon as I fill Ela in, I'll talk to you and Suz."

"Gotcha." Tyler sped through the exit.

Nash took her elbow and propelled her a few feet from the desk. "Ela, did you know Tyler worked on a farm?"

His urgent tone alerted her that something was up. "He worked on a horse farm outside of town, before the pizza delivery job. What's the problem?"

"The person who created your bomb used ammonia nitrate. It's common in fertilizer. The police looked into Tyler's background and found that the men at the farm used ammonia nitrate to blow out stumps in the fields this past fall."

"They believe he set off the explosion in our house? I can't imagine Tyler created a bomb."

"It's not a Mensa project. How are he and Suz getting along?"

Ela heaved a sigh. "While you were with your client, Suz told me she and Tyler were leaving Rockypoint together." Tyler tied to the blast didn't feel right. "Nash, I don't think Tyler planted and ignited the bomb. He's not a big planner beyond his takeout orders. Do the police have proof?"

"Except for the connection to the farm, they've nothing else on him. That's the reason they released him, but Ballard's not done. If Tyler bought the ingredients used in the homemade blast, he's in trouble."

"Suz is with him outside."

Ela and Nash walked to the exit. On the sidewalk, she halted and searched for the teens. Where were they? "How did they disappear so quickly?"

Ela's chest tightened. She pulled out her phone, and her heart beat faster and faster with each ring.

Her sister's voicemail answered. "Leave a message."

Ela stopped herself from blurting, "You're with our bomber." What if she was wrong or Suz put her on speaker?

Ela dismissed the warning and recited her plea, "Call me right away."

CHAPTER 16

Nash insisted that Ela stay at his place and wait for Suz to text or call instead of going to her house.

"You can't follow me around forever," Ela told him as they walked from the station to his car. "Suz is the one who needs attention and should be locked away until she's forty. What about your job? You should be in your office on a Friday afternoon."

"Once you're settled, I'll return to work. Lanie's at school, and then she'll be at my mother's until I pick her up tomorrow." He guided Ela toward his car as he spoke.

"Suz was mad at me. She must have gone off with Tyler."

Nash hit unlock on the key chain. "You still need to play it safe. I'll check for Suz at your place before I head downtown."

Within the next thirty minutes, he settled Ela into his home and set off again to do a quick run-through of the Victorian. With no signs of Suz at the house, he grabbed his phone and reported his lack of findings to Ela. After offering reassurances, Nash pulled up findaaronwright's webpage on his phone. He scrolled to the bottom and found a comment in response to his last post bashing Aaron.

"Fed Up, you should know the truth. Aaron Wright was an innocent victim. May he rest in peace. Learn the facts before you cast the first stone. I remain dedicated to Aaron."

"You can do better than a friend who was a thief," Nash typed. "Aaron threw enough stones for all of us. He made the trusting and naive his targets. Do not defend a guilty man." Nash signed the message the same as the last: *Fed Up.*

Finished, Nash ran through his contacts and punched the button next to his investigator Jake's name. Nash directed him to send info on the federal agent in charge of the Blanchette fraud investigation and reminded their techie they were expecting his report.

After reassurances, Nash hung up and set off for the courthouse where he was assisting his dad in a jury selection. The rest of the day flew. At the dinner break, he called Ela. "I'll be finished in another hour or two. Any word?"

"I haven't heard from Suz, yet. I was beginning to think Tyler cared for her and wouldn't hurt her, but taking off like this has changed my mind. I'm going to talk to Ballard."

Her voice sounded low and tired. "Good. We can't take risks."

"It's possible that she went to our house to pick up a change of clothes after you stopped by. Suz wouldn't care about a missing front door as long as she could lock her bedroom. I'll take a taxi home."

"Stay where you are. If you hear from Suz, call me immediately. Don't open up for anyone except her."

"I've had nothing to do but search the internet for news about teenagers, and I appreciate you lending a hand, but you've already done so much."

"We take care of each other in Rockypoint. It's part of the code."

"You're making that up."

"You'll find out. Help yourself to any eatable food in the fridge. See you soon."

"Okay."

The disappointment in her voice told him she wasn't happy. He hung up and pressed the number from his contact list.

Darkness had fallen by the time Nash left the courthouse. The beep of his phone alerted him to the message as he walked to the lot. He unlocked his car and jumped inside before reading the new text.

Done.

The outside light shone over his front door when he arrived, and Ela greeted him at his front step. He took one look at her face and gave her a hug.

"I'm so worried about my sister. Chief Ballard put out a BOLA for Suz, but he's more interested in arresting Tyler."

"We'll find her." He released Ela and walked into the hall. "Did you eat?"

"I couldn't swallow a bite." Her mouth tightened.

She needed good news. "Ready to go home?"

"Prison guards couldn't keep me away."

They rode in silence to the Victorian. As she got out of his vehicle, her phone buzzed. She paused to answer. "My sister sent me a text." A smile of relief lit her face. "She says she'll be home soon."

"Did she give you a hint where she was?"

Ela shook her head. "At least she's not hurt. I'll never have kids unless I can send them away when they hit double digits."

He put his arm around her shoulders and tugged her against his side. She leaned into him for a second, and he felt her gathering strength, squaring her shoulders.

She pulled away. "I'm ready to straighten up my house."

They walked up the front steps in unison, until she paused on the top stair. "Someone tacked a note to the door. Wait—how'd we get a door?"

"Read the letter." He tugged the paper free and handed it to her.

Dear Ela and Suz:

We heard you needed a little cleanup at your home. We were happy to help. Your neighbors.

"I barely know my neighbors." She looked at him with wonder in her eyes. "Nash, you did this. I can tell by the expression on your face."

"What? My face never gives away my thoughts. Ask a jury."

"I'll pass for now. Who fixed the door? I want to thank them."

"My father contacted the rotary, and my mother organized her women's group. The window where your intruder entered in the rear is taken care of, too. They installed a new one with grids. No one will crawl through unless they shrink to fly size."

"I never expected such a gift. I'll need their names to repay them."

"Forget it. Give me the keys."

She passed him the key, and he unlocked the deadbolts. They stepped into the hall, and he flipped on the lights.

"My gate-leg table is together." She blinked back tears. "Who'd guess I'd long for Aunt Vickie's furniture? If only the vase hadn't shattered." She shook her head, peeked into the parlor and froze. "The place is spotless." She whirled toward him. "How will I repay the people who helped me?"

He took her hands in his. "Two words—thank you."

She opened her mouth to protest.

"Repeat after me. Thank you."

"Thank you?"

"Better. And I've one more idea about how to show your gratitude."

"Do I have to parrot you again?"

"You should." He lowered his mouth to her lips and caught the warm gasp of her breath. He pulled her against his chest. The zipper pull on her fleece pressed against his shirt through his open jacket. Her lips were as sweet as the honey in his coffee, and tucked against him, she felt small and fragile. He loosened his hold and cupped her chin in his hand. Her gaze locked onto his. "Why are you so good to me?" she asked.

"If you don't know, I must not have done a good job of kissing you."

"I'll vouch for your abilities." A teasing light sparkled in her eyes.

"To make sure you understood one of my reasons for helping you, we better try again." He brushed his lips across her cheek and nibbled at her chin.

She laid a restraining hand on his chest and stepped away from him. "How you or I kiss is one thing we don't have to worry about. We should concentrate on Suz and the rest of the house."

"Gotcha. No more distractions." He repressed a sigh and the desire to pull her back into his arms. Together they breezed through the parlor and into the kitchen, calling Suz's name. She wasn't home.

Ela glanced at her phone in her hand.

"Checking for messages is as exciting as watching grass grow," Nash said to her.

She sighed, slipped into a chair and hit the numbers for Suz's phone. After five rings, her sister's voicemail answered, "Leave a message."

"Suz, I need you to call me right away."

Ela clicked off her cell and sat, tapping her fingers. "I keep remembering the pastor's words when he visited the hospital. He said it's easy to have faith in the good times. It's so true."

He slid into the seat beside her. "I can pray for you if you wish."

She bit her lip. "I'll do it myself." She grasped his hand tight. "Please watch over Suz," she whispered. "Keep her safe and bring her home soon."

She glanced down at her phone, lying on the table in front of her.

"It doesn't work instantaneously."

"I was just hoping."

"Hope is good. It gets us to faith."

She nodded. "Suz is probably de-stressing somewhere."

He wrapped his arm around her shoulders, and she leaned against him. The familiar scent of lavender curled around them.

"Nash, maybe I made her go away by arguing with her."

"Suz knows you love her."

"I loved my father, and I sent him to jail." She pulled away from him, clasping and unclasping her hands. "I stay awake night after night and ask myself what kind of daughter am I?"

A jolt of surprise rocked Nash, but he grasped hold of his court training and remained calm. "Want to talk about it?"

"If you'll listen." She stared over his shoulder, avoiding his gaze. "My father kept two financial books. One day when I started to close down his computer, I found his true figures. He probably thought he'd closed the program, but he'd only minimized the page when he left in a rush for a meeting. I reported him to the police after a lot of conscience wrestling, but I learned he'd already attracted the attention of the Federal Trade Commission. My call sped up his arrest, not started the investigation. I hold onto that detail to remind myself I'm not totally responsible for his downfall."

"You followed your sense of right and wrong."

"My father was big time wrong. He was a thief and guilty of

hurting plenty of people." She shoved her hair back from her face before continuing. "The prosecution agreed to keep me out of court since they had plenty of evidence against him. But the fact remains, I helped imprison my father."

"Ela—"

"Then I encouraged the plea bargain. I believed he should be punished, but the deal seemed fair," she interjected. "When my dad went before the judge, he rejected the plea, stating my father had committed the worst offense by knowingly ruining the lives of those who trusted him."

"Your father was a grown man, responsible for himself. Don't play the blame game."

"I should have looked for a lawyer with experience that matched the magnitude of his crimes. Maybe then his plea would have been accepted. Other days I ask myself why didn't I keep quiet? How could I turn in my own parent?" Pain creased her face.

"The right course of action isn't always easy," Nash said in a gentle voice.

"And now Suz is missing. If anything happens to her—" Ela's voice broke.

"She'll come home soon." He squeezed her hand.

"I wish I had your confidence, but she does operate on Suz time." Ela fidgeted with the cuff of her shirt. "Can you—"

Leave, he added mentally.

"—stay awhile?"

"I thought you'd never ask."

* * *

Money Bags would call soon. Yeah, the bomb was a dud. Well, not a big dud. A picture of the smoke and the fire engines at the Danforth house made the newspaper's front page. What a rush.

But nobody would read an obit. He shifted in his bucket seat to stretch his legs. When he got cash, he'd buy a cool car. He'd tell Money Bags this one got stolen and sell it to a chop shop.

His phone rang. Yup. Money was calling to yell at him.

"Meet me at the usual place and time, and no tails," Money Bags ordered.

"The bomb was a good idea. I just needed a little more ammo."

"We'll talk." Money's voice softened. "I've a new proposal for you."

"I don't want to change the plan. I told ya, I was just playing with them. I've got the big ending mapped in my head."

Money blew a breath into the receiver. "Tonight. Meet me."

He didn't want Money to forget the extra cash, especially since he might be backing out. "I'll take the bonus now."

"When the job's done. Get on it." He clicked off.

He had a few hours to come up with the grand scheme that would knock Money Bags' pants off. He snorted. He'd love to see that.

* * *

Ela made three batches of fudge before she fell asleep on the settee. She woke with a start and sat up. "Suz?"

"Sorry." Nash stood in front of her with two cups of coffee in his hands.

She rubbed her eyes. "What time is it?"

"It's seven. You slept an hour." He set the mugs on the coffee table.

She sat upright. "I'm not sure what to do next."

"Call the Rawlings. She could be at Tyler's house." He held out a scrap of paper. "I found their number while you were sleeping."

"Thanks." She scooped up her phone. Her hands shook as she hit the numbers.

A nasal-voiced woman answered and identified herself as Mrs. Rawlings. Ela explained the situation and tightened her grip on her cell until Mrs. Rawlings said she'd hadn't seen Suz.

Ela hung up and shook her head at Nash. She struggled to swallow the disappointment clogging her throat. "I'm calling Chief Ballard again."

Nash sat beside her. His hand on her knee reassured Ela, and kept her fears under control while she listened to the chief's phone ring.

"Ballard."

Ela poured out her concerns, and he agreed to send someone to the Rawlings place. "Tyler and Suz could be holed up at their house," he acknowledged. "A lot of parents are afraid to go into their kids' rooms. Disappearing seems to be a habit with your sister."

"My sister was mad and said she was moving out, but she usually gets over her anger in a few minutes."

"Can you think of a friend who'd let her stay with him or her?"

Ela searched her memory. "She mentioned Dylan once. I don't know his last name. He was a friend of Tyler's." This was getting them nowhere. Ela tapped her foot on the floor. "We've been over these questions. I'm going to speak to the principal at her school."

"You stay put in case she comes home. Contact me if she does. I'll take care of the interviews." Ballard hung up.

"He wasn't much help," she said in answer to Nash's questioning look. "I'd love for Suz to walk in and criticize my clothes, my hair, or my life right now. What kind of sister am I? She always said Tyler was her only friend at school, but she might have been exaggerating. She could be with someone I never met."

"We'll find her. And you're a caring sister." He glanced at his watch. "I'm sorry. I need to explain to my parents why Lanie should sleep over tonight."

"Nash, you can't sit around with me. You promised Lanie you'd pick her up and bring her home. You can't disappoint her." Ela couldn't be responsible for keeping Nash from his daughter. "You should spend every possible minute with her while she wants you around and that includes this evening."

"I don't like the idea of you in the house alone. Come with me."

"I'm safe, thanks to your family and friends. I can't rest if you don't see Lanie because of me."

He kissed her and held her for a second before speaking. "I'll go, for now. When Suz returns, call me."

She walked him to the door, and he kissed her, making her head reel.

"I'll hurry back," he whispered in her ear, sending a ripple of anticipation through her. He grabbed his jacket from the closet. "Remember, keep the door locked."

When he reached his car, he waved and then took off. She flicked the deadbolt. From the other room, her phone rang. She ran into the parlor and scooped it up from the coffee table.

A warning whispered in her head: *Ignore the call.*

She shut out the caution until Caller ID confirmed it was him. She was done. Her throat tightened as she hit the talk button.

"Return, O Lord, and rescue me."

"Hello, Dad."

CHAPTER 17

"Calling hours at the prison ended an hour ago. I told you not to call me, especially not on an illegal cell." Ela gripped her phone.

"I'll accept the consequences, Michaela. I'm worried about you. I want us to meet again in the afterlife."

Her stomach cramped, and she bit back a retort about where he'd be in the afterlife. "Dad, I know you've found comfort in the Bible, but don't lecture me on *my* soul."

"I never see you. You never write. Your sister and mother mail me letters. *You* cut me off."

"I'll send money. You'll need some once you've done your punishment for the illicit calls. You know they'll track your signal." Irritation ripped through her. He always pretended concern for her before he couched his request for funds in scriptures. He didn't care about her, Suz or their mother, only money.

"I could use a few dollars for cigarettes."

She'd guessed, but the truth didn't stop the stab that made her flinch. She counted each breath until she could speak. "I'll arrange it."

"Bring the cash when you visit."

"I can't, Dad. I'll wire it to your lawyer."

"I've a new one. He prays for me every day."

"Good. Have him contact me."

"He's writing an appeal. He thinks we'll win."

"They all say that, Dad. They want what's left of your pennies."

"He prays for you and Suz, too."

"We're fine. Don't bother."

"Come visit."

"I can't."

"You sit in a room on one side of a glass. We talk over a phone. Do it for me."

Her life was in ruins because of him. The anger in her chest began to bubble.

"You should come see me here," her father continued. "They nicknamed me Preacher and move away when I walk through the halls. I'd rather they talked to me."

She didn't want to speak to him either. "Good bye, Dad."

"Don't hang up. How's Suz?"

Ela reigned in her temper. "I have to go. Speak to me through your lawyer. Don't call me again."

"I love you, Ela."

The soft voice and words were from the father she loved. Her thumb hovered over the end button. The words clogged in her throat. "You were my hero, Dad," she whispered, and she disconnected.

She'd never escape him and his actions. "You were supposed to protect me." A tear ran down her cheek. She closed her eyes and prayed for him.

A strange serenity filled her after the moment of silent appeal. She was done waiting and sitting around until she became an antique. She'd find Suz. First, she'd head over to the Rawlings. Take a taxi or rent a car, she'd get there. She raced upstairs, showered and changed into clean jeans and a green blouse.

She ran downstairs and booted up her laptop on the coffee table. Taxi, taxi. They must exist in Rockypoint. Ah, she found one. She hit the digits on her keypad and fired off her address to the dispatch. Scooping up her purse, she dug out the key to lock up.

"Suz, wherever you are, I'm coming." Ela stood at the bay window, peeking out of the blackout curtains, watching for her ride.

The house phone rang. She crossed the carpet and grabbed the receiver.

"Miss Danforth, this is Chief Byron Jones of the Rockypoint

Fire Department. We're at your store because a passing motorist reported smoke escaping from your building."

Outside, a car horn tooted.

"I'm on my way."

"Hang on a minute. If it's a false alarm, our engine may be gone when you arrive but I'll stay to fill you in."

She pressed the end button, raced to the cab and directed the driver to the store. If Now and Then burned, a large sum of money would go up in smoke with it.

The cabbie sped off. The traffic was light, and he turned onto the shop's street in minutes. He stopped at the curb. "Are you sure this is the place?"

She couldn't criticize him for asking. "Yes, you can go." She paid the man, registering that he stared at her for several seconds as though he expected her to change her mind. He left with a squeal of tires.

Ela clutched her key and scanned her store in the light of the street lamps for smoke or flames. Nothing. She sniffed the air. The scent of rotting garbage assaulted her senses. She started forward. The fire chief should be nearby. No signs of anyone moving around in the closed, dark building. Something wasn't right.

Across the street, the tattoo store was opening. She hit Nash's number and hung up when she heard his voicemail. She'd handle this without taking him away from Lanie. Chief Ballard came up on her contact list. He answered on the second ring, and in one rush, she explained what had happened.

"Sit tight. I'm on it."

At the sound of an engine, she glanced over her shoulder. Tyler parked at the curb and hopped out. "Is Suz here?"

"She's not..." Ela's breath deserted her, and then returned in quick gasps. "with you?"

"She was for a while. We rode around to talk about if we should leave or stay in Rockypoint. But we ended up fighting. When I slowed for the stop sign near your place, Suz jumped out. She said she'd walk home, and told me to get lost."

"You left her alone? When?" Ela fought the panic rising in the back of her throat.

"It was about twenty minutes ago. I just rode around until I cooled down and went back to where I'd last seen her. She wasn't around. I figured she'd made it home. I stopped at your house. No one was there. That's when I came here, looking for Suz." He peered closer at her. "You don't look good. Your face is black and blue."

Ela shook her head and wrapped her arms around herself as a cool breeze gushed on the street. "Forget my face. What did Suz say when you left the police station?"

"She told me you wanted to lock her up forever."

Ela clamped her mouth shut and marched toward the building. Could Suz be inside, hiding? "She sent me a text hours ago that she'd be home soon."

"I...I didn't know about it," he said, tagging along behind her. "Is she in the store?"

"I'll look." Ela turned the key. The memory of the front door of her house blowing up forced her to retreat. "I called the police. Maybe we should wait for them."

"I'll do it." Tyler swooped in front of her and yanked.

"No!"

The door flew open. A body tumbled out and landed at Ela's feet. A package of Octopus gum plopped on the ground.

CHAPTER 18

Ela crouched beside the body. His lanky form and scarred cheek gave him away. Mr. SOC! She laid a finger on the spot in his neck where a pulse should beat. She leaped back. "He's gone."

"It's Dylan."

"You know him?" Was Tyler kidding?

"We worked together on the farm last summer. Suz and I were planning to share an apartment with him when we first talked about moving in together. I can't believe it."

"Me either. Your Dylan could be our stalker." She pointed at the gum.

"Suz told me about the wrappers in your garage. Everyone chews Octopus." Tyler rubbed a hand over his face. "Poor Dylan."

Ela leaned over the deceased and yelled into the open doorway, "Suz! Suz, are you in there?" *Please be okay.*

No one answered. Ela's stomach cramped with fear.

"I'll go look." Tyler started forward.

"No." She grabbed his arm. Just then she spotted Ballard's car. "There's the chief."

The detective parked in front of Tyler's compact and marched over to them. He halted as his gaze fell on Mr. SOC.

Ela recounted the events leading up to their discovery of Dylan, aka Mr. SOC, as Ballard bent over the dead man. Shock loosened its grip on her. She averted her gaze and concentrated on breathing over the nausea growing in her stomach.

"It's Dylan French," Tyler added. "Just because he chews Octopus Eight doesn't make him a stalker."

"When I mentioned Mr. SOC's limp, Dylan didn't come to mind?" Ela asked? Tyler knew her tormenter all this time?

"Dylan said his leg would heal. When you freaked over the guy grabbing you, I thought of some old guy with a useless leg."

Ela blew out a breath of frustration.

"Did he have a heart attack or something?" Tyler began to pace, his mouth compressed by shock.

Ballard checked Mr. SOC's vital signs. "What are you doing here, Rawlings?" he said, as he straightened to pull out his phone.

Tyler paused and ran a hand through his hair. "I was driving around and stopped to talk to Ela."

"You just happened to be driving past. Where's Suz Danforth?" Ballard fastened cold eyes on the teen.

"I'm searching for her, too. She'll be blown away when she finds out Dylan's dead." Tyler gulped loudly. "I can't believe he's gone either."

"Looks like a bullet went through his chest." Ballard said.

Ela twisted the ring on her finger. "He's the man from the hospital, and I believe the one on the security tape at my house."

"Both of you go wait by your car while I look around."

Ballard's order sounded perfect since Ela didn't want to go into the building at the moment. A man was dead. In her store. Was Suz inside, injured or...worse?

She tugged Tyler to his car, and leaned against the hood for support.

"Chief Ballard suspects me of killing Dylan." Tyler walked in a small circle on the sidewalk and paused. "No one will believe me, except Suz, and I lost her."

The anguish in his voice stirred Ela's sympathy. "I believe you, Tyler, and we'll find Suz. Don't worry."

"You mean it?" he asked in a broken whisper.

Ela paused, but the truth wouldn't go away. "Yes. Would Suz go off with Dylan?"

"If he wanted to show her an apartment, she might, but Suz never went off with him alone before." Tyler sniffed. "I don't understand what happened to him or Suz."

"Where did you meet Dylan, again?" Ela glanced over at the still form on the threshold. Nerves made her hands unsteady, and she clasped them together to keep them still. She turned to Tyler to block out the sight of the dead man.

"We met on the farm last summer, and this spring, he was looking for a job cuz they didn't need him anymore. Suz's gotta be okay. I love her." Tyler covered his face with his palms and broke into tears.

His anguish propelled Ela forward, and she put her palm on his shaking shoulder. "We'll locate her, but you need to hold it together."

He raised his red-streaked face. "How do you know?"

"Because we have faith that the good guys will win." The words fell out of her mouth and felt natural and right.

"Ela!"

* * *

Nash leaned out his open car window and parked in a spot across the street. In two strides, he was beside her. The crinkle in her forehead warned him something terrible was going on.

"What happened?" He searched her face for an answer.

"Fire Chief Byron phoned and informed me smoke was coming out of my building."

"Rockypoint doesn't have a Fire Chief Byron."

"I learned that. Tyler arrived a few minutes later, and when we opened the door, we found his friend Dylan, or Mr. SOC, dead. A package of Octopus gum fell out of his pocket."

"SOC was your stalker *and* a friend of Tyler's?" What was going on?

She filled him in on Tyler, Suz and Mr. SOC, aka Dylan. "Tyler and Suz say everyone chews the gum. How did you find me?"

"My father organized his men's group into a watch. One of them saw you leaving, tailed you and called dad while I was at their house with Lanie."

"I should give you a lecture about leaving your daughter, and I'm ignoring the whole group watch thing, for now, though I guess I owe them a thanks."

"I told Lanie Suz was missing, and she asked me to help bring her best friend home. I couldn't argue with her." He inclined his head. "I noticed Ballard's black SUV."

"He's looking around the store for Suz. I pray she's not in there." Ela folded her arms and held onto her elbows while her body shook.

"She'll be okay," he affirmed.

"Nobody knows where Suz is," Tyler cried from the curb. He smashed his fist against his other palm. "The police shouldn't have kept me at the station. She was too upset for me to calm her down when I was released."

"There's a camera outside the police station," Nash said. "Maybe someone followed when you left with Suz, and we can ID the person or car's plate number from the surveillance."

"That would be great." Tyler's voice lifted with hope.

Ballard's men started to arrive. The chief shouted directions, and the officers scurried in and around Now and Then, taping off the area. Men tugged on latex gloves and placed plastic covers over their shoes to enter the crime scene.

Nash faced Tyler. "We'll meet you at Ela's. If Suz is home, call me." Nash spouted off his number.

Tyler hit the digits into his phone. "Okay, wait at Suz's. Call if she's home." He hopped into his compact and zoomed off.

When Tyler's car disappeared, Nash turned to find Ballard stomping toward him.

"Where's that kid going?" Ballard demanded. "I told him to stay with his car so we could do our jobs."

"He's with his car."

"Don't play me, McCain. I'll arrest you right here."

"What's the charge? I advised my client to allow the police to do their work."

"He was at the scene of a possible homicide. I want to interview him."

"That's why he's my client."

"Chief." Ela moved closer to him. "Have your men finished canvassing my store? Any sign of Suz?"

"No one's inside. I'll send an officer to your house to interview you later." He compressed his lips into a hard line. "And if you see the kid at your house, tell him to not to leave."

"Thank you, Chief."

"Any chance of a security camera outside the station that

would capture someone following Tyler Rawlings yesterday?" Nash asked, ready to head out.

"The station's surveillance is monitored day and night. No suspicious person or vehicle tailed anyone yesterday or I'd be the first one on it. Now if you're done playing detective, McCain, I'll return to my job."

Ela met Nash's gaze. "Let's go."

When they arrived at the Victorian, Nash pointed out the obvious. "Tyler's not here. Guess he didn't listen to me."

"I don't think he listens to anyone, but he does seem to care about my sister. His tears seemed genuine. I hope Suz didn't take a ride from Dylan. How can we find her, Nash?"

"Let's decide what to do when we're settled inside." They trekked to the porch, where they both stopped at the sight of a piece of paper anchored down by a rock on the top step.

"Don't touch it," Nash warned as she reached for it.

She bent over the message. "Left to find Suz. T."

Ela straightened. "Too bad he didn't write where he was going."

"Tyler doesn't make life easy," Nash agreed. "I'll pick up the note in a few minutes.

Let's go into the parlor first." Nash held out his hand for the house key. She stood back while he unlocked and opened the door.

"Wait here while I scout around." He entered and walked through the rooms, where he unearthed nothing unusual. In the kitchen, he found a box of plastic baggies and grabbed one. The house was secure. He strode back to Ela standing in the open doorway. "No one's here. Come on in."

Ela's phone rang as she entered. She glanced at the caller ID and ended the call.

Nash went onto the porch and scooped the note and rock into the plastic bag and locked the baggie in his car, just in case Ballard wanted it. Back in the house, he approached Ela in the hallway. "Was your sister on the phone?"

She shook her head and sagged against the door jamb. "It was my father, who's in jail."

"Matt Blanchette phoned you?" Why hadn't he asked if she was in contact with her father? He'd always assumed the upsetting calls she'd rejected were from Aaron and that he must be disguising his voice, or out of a false loyalty, she wouldn't admit he was her harasser. He was striking out big time today. "Has he heard from Suz?"

"No." Her voice roughened, and she scooted across the hall and into the parlor.

"Did you ask him?" Nash persisted, following her. "During their calls, Suz might have mentioned a place she liked to go or a friend we should talk to."

Ela wheeled around, her hands on her hips. "My father and I spoke the other day. Suz writes him but she hasn't seen him since New York and never mentions visiting him. He phones me for one reason. He wants to save my soul in return for money."

"Talk to him about your sister."

"No."

"Ela, he ought to know she's missing. He's still her father and yours."

"I'm not in the mood for reminders about families or sharing problems." She threw out her arms and raised her chin. "I can't forget he's my parent. It's a fact that never changes. He's also a cheat, and a liar and ruined people's lives."

"You need to—"

"Forgive him?"

"I was going to say move on, but yes, forgiveness is part of the deal. You're not responsible for your father's faults, but he deserves a second chance."

"Thanks for the sermon, McCain. Have you moved on? Is that why you saved your wife's clothes, haven't bought new furniture—or changed your home since she died?"

"What?" He felt a muscle jump in his cheek.

"You have a daughter who spends more time with your parents than with you. Your wife died two years ago, but you keep the master bedroom exactly as she decorated it and won't use it for yourself. And you lecture me about my family relationships."

"I didn't realize the way I led my life bothered you." He shifted away, her assessment of him chafing against his self-respect. He'd misjudged the strength of his bond with Ela. He'd right his mistake now. "We all have a past, but I understand if you prefer not to hear my history." He walked to the door and paused. "I'll speak to the man who was on the neighborhood watch. I'll contact you if I learn anything about Suz. Otherwise, I won't bother you."

The door closed, and the house echoed with silence.

* * *

A pang of regret flooded through her as she crossed the floor to the window. Nash's sports car pulled out of the driveway and disappeared from view.

She curled and uncurled her fingers. Remorse nagged at her to call him. How could she fix what she'd done? The simple words *I'm sorry* didn't heal. Her father uttered the meaningless phrase hundreds of times. What could she say?

Her phone rang. She grabbed it. "Suz? Nash?"

"Ah, no, this is Kevin, your realtor. I emailed you the contract for the estate sale. Did you read and sign the papers yet?"

"I'll send the agreement over tomorrow." She put the phone down.

She sat on the settee in the quiet of the house. As in the days when she'd lost everything in New York, she was alone.

The rear doorbell rang. Nash? She sprinted through the house and paused to glance at the camera's screen on the wall and then peeked out the window for a better view. The outdoor light revealed her visitor, a tall, blond haired man in the familiar Italian leather jacket. Her heart sped up.

Aaron!

* * *

Nash's emotions swirled underneath his skin while he cruised for ten minutes on autopilot before the hospital came into view. He pulled into the lot and parked. Here, he'd met Ela for the first time. The memory of her leaning against the nursery glass with a wistful look sharpened in his mind.

More than anything, he wanted to call her, but he wasn't sure how to restore their relationship.

His phone went off. "McCain."

"Ah, Nash, this is Tyler, Suz's boyfriend."

"Where did you go? We were supposed to meet at the Danforth house."

"I left a note. I've been driving around looking for Suz. I can't find her."

"Tyler, would she go to New York?"

"I doubt it. She didn't like it there. I'm going by the school." He hung up.

He wasn't much help. Nash's phone rang again. The caller ID revealed his dad was on the other end. Nash answered and summed up the events for him. "Suz might have gone to visit her father in New York. He's her only family besides Ela in the US. I'll call Uncle John. It's a long shot that she left the state, but if she did, we don't want a young girl hanging out at a top-security prison."

"Agreed. If she's on the road hitching rides, she's in danger. I'll notify the state police."

"The Danforth house is safe. I'll call a security company to install new cameras A.S.A.P. The front one was blown off by the blast and the rear one should be replaced since the picture quality is poor. Both were ancient."

"Lanie called to ask if you'd found her friend, yet."

"Lanie called you from school?"

"She did. Seems a friend lent her a cell phone at recess. I think she wanted to try it, more than speak to me."

"Okay, Dad. I'll be in the office soon. I want to find out if Ballard canvassed the bus and taxi stations for Suz."

After they disconnected, Nash phoned his uncle in New York and explained the situation.

"I'll check with the prison," Uncle John answered. "Any possibility she'd visit Aaron's family or her mother?"

"Good idea. We should cover all avenues. I believe Suz doesn't know her mom's specific whereabouts in Europe. If you'd alert the Wrights, we'd be covered. I appreciate your help." Nash left the lot and continued toward the police station. The news about Lanie's unusual call nagged him. His father had said a friend loaned her the cell phone. Who was this friend? The girl who never attended a sleepover, birthday party or hung out at a schoolmate's house had a friend's cell phone.

The answer hit him. Nash u-turned at the next side street. A short distance from home, he parked and jogged the rest of the way.

The sounds of the television greeted him as he walked through the front door. Nash crept into the TV room and stopped. Suz dozed in the recliner. Across the hardwood floor, the commercial blared out a onetime offer for a dirt-eating vacuum.

"Suz."

She startled awake and glanced about the room until she focused on him. "Nash." She clicked the chair into its upright position. She grabbed the remote and turned off the ad. "You're supposed to be at work."

"What are you doing in my house?"

"I...I broke in because I don't have a home anymore. I'm on my own." She averted her face and rose. "I'll go."

"Stay where you are. Your sister almost killed herself trying to find you."

Suz angled her head to the side as though judging his truthfulness. "You're exaggerating."

"Someone lured her to Now and Then. When Ela arrived, hoping you were there, she discovered a dead body. There's a chance the killer was waiting inside to hurt or threaten her, but was scared off by the police."

Suz blinked several times. "Is Ela okay?"

"She's shaken up. If you went home, she'd feel a lot better."

Suz shook her head. "Who died?"

"Tyler showed up and ID'd him. He's your friend and possibly your stalker, Dylan French."

"Dylan?" Her eyes widened. "Tyler must be upset. They were friends. I barely knew him." She sank into the chair. "Dylan was the stalker and Tyler was with Ela? Lots has been going on since I left."

"Ela's home pacing the floor, hoping you'll show up, and Tyler's searching the town for you."

Suz slumped forward. "I can't go home. I broke up with Tyler and told Ela I was leaving forever."

"Your sister wants you to come back. I bet Tyler does too."

Suz sighed. "I'll call her."

"And I'll talk to your co-conspirator, Lanie."

Suz's mouth dropped open. "She didn't have anything to do with me holing up here."

"She encouraged you to hide in our home, and you reciprocated by lending Lanie your phone."

"Coming here was my idea. Lanie showed me where you stashed the extra key outside and how to turn off the alarm when I babysat. I decided to hang out for a while until I figured where to go next."

"How did you get here?"

"I hold onto Tyler's tips for future rent money. I used them to pay for a taxi." She dug into her pocket and came up with a five and a one. "This is what's left. Can you give it to him?"

"You do it."

"I—we said awful things to each other."

"That's why we have apologies." His own words sank in. He should take his own advice. "I'll reset the code. If you decide to phone Tyler, don't let him know you're at my house. Whoever wants to harm you could follow him. We need to keep your location secret."

"You mean Dead Man's Curve and the explosion weren't accidents?"

"No, Suz." Nash turned to leave the room.

She trudged along behind him. "Moose Hill seemed like an accident. If Ela hadn't stayed home from her book club that night, I wouldn't have gone out."

He faced her, blocking her. "Ela was supposed to drive the night you went off the curve?"

"Yup. She changed her mind about going at the last minute, and I took the car. But the members of her club wouldn't stalk anyone unless they were Jane Austen." She rolled her eyes.

Ela should have been driving when Suz crashed. "She's home alone!" He grabbed his cell and hit her number. Her phone rang until voicemail answered.

He disconnected. "Suz, I want you to stay at my parents. Ready?"

"Is Ela okay?"

"I don't know."

CHAPTER 19

"Aaron." Ella raced to answer the bell while her mind shouted, *He's dead*. She flung the door open. "Aar—"

"Thank you, Michaela, for the warm greeting."

Up close, strands of white hair stood out in his blond head. Wrinkles lined his forehead.

The over six-foot male in the navy nylon jacket and jeans wasn't Aaron. She'd never seen this man dressed in such casual clothing. Her brain whirled, trying to make sense of it. "Judge Wright? What are you doing in Rockypoint?"

"Can I come in? We need to talk." He placed one large foot on the threshold and prevented her from shutting the door.

Something big had happened. Judge Wright wouldn't leave his home or job to chat. Her adrenaline level shot upward. "Is it about Aaron?"

He brushed past her into the kitchen without answering.

She trailed behind him unable to shake her uneasiness. "I didn't recognize you. I thought you were…Aaron."

"I'm wearing his jacket." A vein pulsed at the base of his throat as he faced her. "Aaron's brother, Ray, was killed in a hit and run accident last month."

She drew in a sharp breath. "I'm sorry."

The Judge sank into a chair and hung his head. What was going on? The Judge never acted dejected or grief stricken. Throughout the ordeal with Aaron, he was the one who'd cheered the family with words of hope and action. Even his cool persona at Aaron's memorial was nothing like the man before her. She barely recognized him. Unease rubbed against her nerves.

She gripped her hands together and inched further from him. "Did the accident happen near Rockypoint? Is that why you're here?"

"No." He jerked his head upward and glared.

The anger in his voice sent a shiver of wariness up her spine. She tried again to override her discomfort. "Is your wife in Rockypoint?"

"I came to discuss Aaron."

They must have found his body. Her mouth went dry. "Did Ray learn more about Aaron before he was hit?"

"No." The judge's eyes glowed with a strange light.

Something was wrong with him. Her discomfort morphed into fright, warning her to get away from him. "You should come back later when we can talk in private. I'm expecting company." She gestured to the door, eager for him to leave.

He stood and blocked her path with his broad chest. "Don't you want to hear why I'm here? Don't you care about my family?" His powerful hands fisted by his sides.

Her stomach churned with nerves. From the parlor came the ring of her cell phone. "I have to answer. My sister Suz is missing. It might be her."

He clenched his jaw, and his face reddened as he towered over her. "Not now."

Panic boomeranged in her chest, and she backed away. He seized her forearms in an iron grip, setting free her terror. "You ruined his life. You killed Aaron."

"Me?" Was the Judge crazy? "Aaron drowned."

"You and your dad were crooks, but you both survived. Your father sits in a country club prison and you live in a huge house in suburbia while Aaron floated in a watery grave until sharks ripped him apart. He was my son." He shrieked the last word, and his fingers dug deeper and bruised her skin. "I—will—have—justice."

She struggled to break free. "Let go."

"It's too late, Michaela."

He yanked her across the room as if she were a toddler. She shot a kick at him and lost her balance. Abruptly, he released her and she hit the floor with a whack to her skull. Stunned, she didn't react when he grabbed her foot, dragging her into the parlor, where he picked her up and tossed her on the settee.

He stabbed a finger at her. "If Aaron never met *you*, he'd be alive today."

She shook her head. "I never hurt Aaron." *Talk him down.*

"No more lies." He drew a gun from his pocket.

Sweat broke out and soaked her clothes. He aimed the muzzle at her chest.

"Don't shoot." She held up her hands. "Aaron's alive. He's alive!"

* * *

"Your sister's not answering." Nash clicked off his cell. "I'm taking you to my parents' house. You'll be safer there, Suz."

"Is my sister in trouble?"

"I don't know. I'll call Ballard and ask him to head over to your place. He might get there before I do."

"Forget Officer Grump. I'm going with you."

The worry in the back of Nash's mind grew. The buzz of his phone alerted him to a text.

"I'll grab my backpack in the kitchen and then I'll be ready." Suz ran out of the room.

Nash pulled up the message and the last sentence from his techie caught his attention. The emails posted on findaaronwright.com had been sent from the Rockypoint Public Library.

The poster was in the building where Ela worked. He'd been watching her the whole time and could be their bomber and more. Nash's phone rang as soon as he finished reading. "Ela?"

"It's your father again. Mr. Harrington is on a rampage and threatening to transfer his business to a new lawyer who'll accept his calls day or night. You need to talk to him and reassure him he's hired the lawyer of his dreams."

"Tell him I'm busy with a matter of life and death and don't have time for him." Nash ended the conversation.

Suz returned with her backpack. "What's wrong?"

"We're going to check on Ela."

They were a block from his office when his Uncle John rang. Nash answered without slowing the car. "What's the news?"

"I talked with Judge Wright's wife. She said he left for their summer home in Vermont about a month ago after their second son, Raymond, died in a hit and run accident. They still haven't named a suspect in Raymond's death, and her husband's not dealing well. From her description, it sounded like the Judge suffered a breakdown."

"The Judge is in Vermont?" Nash did a quick calculation of how close they were to the border. The new fact sent a warning vibe through his gut. He thanked his uncle and hung up. He hit the accelerator and prayed Ela was safe.

* * *

"Where is he?" The Judge shook Ela.

Her head snapped back and forth. *Help, me, God. Please. Help me.* "Stop. I'll let you know everything."

He tightened his grasp. "Where?"

"Promise you'll leave after I tell you."

His gaze wavered for a second before he nodded.

He was lying.

He let go of her, and she collapsed against the settee and rubbed her arms as she rattled off what he wanted. "Before he disappeared, Aaron believed he'd never beat a guilty verdict. He wouldn't survive jail, so he planned to fake his death and asked me to go with him."

"You're making this up. Aaron wasn't a coward." He spit the last word in her face.

Her whole body shook with fear. She raised her chin and forced out the rest of her story. She had to give herself time. Maybe Suz would show and that would scare him away.

"Aaron wanted to wait for public opinion to calm down and then resurface to deal with the court. I refused to go. I couldn't leave my home, my family. We argued for hours. Finally, he handed over an envelope and told me if I decided to join him, his contact information was inside."

"Aaron told you his destination and you never informed me? You just let me search for him?"

"I never read his letter. I believed if I didn't know where he was, I wasn't part of the scheme. I prayed he wouldn't go through with his idea."

"Where's the letter?"

"I hid it at my aunt's shop. You can get it."

His lip curled with disgust. "You'll go with me."

"I locked it in a canvas trunk near the stairs. I'll get the key." She fisted her hands to hide their shaking.

He yanked her to her feet. His eyes gleamed with a strange light. "Be quick."

The pepper spray was in her coat pocket... "It's in my coat in the front hall closet." Her heart thumped. He hauled her into the hallway and yanked the door open.

Don't search my pockets.

He nudged her forward with the gun.

She slipped her cold hand into the side pocket while he clasped the weapon with both hands a few inches from her. "Can you point that away from me?"

He lowered the barrel toward the floor.

Her fingers closed around the tube. One chance. She whirled around and hit the spray button. He screamed and covered his face with a hand. His firearm discharged in the air. He stumbled against the front door, blocking her escape.

She fled into the parlor. A gunshot whizzed by her ear. Terror pumped through her blood. She sprinted across the floor. Another shot discharged. A burning pain grazed her side. She tripped and fell. *Help, God.* A thousand promises ran through her thoughts.

"Say your final prayers." The Judge loomed over her. Tears streamed from his squinting, red eyes. He leveled the gun on her chest.

Her life was over. She raised her hands in surrender. "Please. Don't."

"Stop!"

Nash stood on the edge of the room. He aimed a weapon at the Judge.

The chief and his team charged in with guns drawn, surrounded and disarmed the Judge. "Are you hurt?" Nash crouched beside her.

Terror still clogged her throat. She managed to shake her head.

Near the sofa, Ballard recited the Miranda rights to the Judge.

"How...did you get in?" she gasped. Was she really safe?

"Through the kitchen. Suz gave me her key. You're bleeding. "I'll drive you to the hospital. Can you stand?"

She nodded and he helped her rise. "You found Suz? Where is she?"

"Ela! Ela!" Suz raced in and threw herself against her sister's shoulder. "I was so scared." She burst into tears.

"You were supposed to stay in the car," Nash said.

"I'm sorry for everything," Suz sobbed.

Ela slid an arm around her sister's waist and kept the other around Nash. She held their breathing, warm bodies close. They were alive, and they were together. She was never letting them go.

CHAPTER 20

A couple of days later, Ela waved good-bye to her sister riding off in Tyler's compact to school. Then, she entered the garage and grabbed the package from the trashcan where Tyler had deposited the mail. The graze had left her sore but mobile. She carried the parcel into the kitchen and set it on the table. From inside, she removed six letters and a Bible. The first three envelopes were addressed to her mother, the next two were for Suz and the last was for her. The message consisted of four sentences. She read them through a blur of tears.

Michaela, you were always the one who followed her conscience when all others stumbled and failed. You are my hero. God Bless. I love you, Dad

A firm knock on the door interrupted her concentration. She wiped her cheeks and stuffed the letters inside the manila envelope on the coffee table. She peeked out the window. Margaret McCain stood on the porch. Ela's hopes rose. She opened up and glanced toward the driveway, searching for the familiar green sports car, but found only Margaret's red hybrid. She'd thanked Nash several times the night of the Judge's attack, but hadn't seen him since. After the cruel words she'd said to him, maybe he never wanted to see her, again. If only she could take them back, but life didn't work that way.

"I hope you don't mind me dropping in," Margaret rushed to say. "You've had so much grief and drama in your life. You probably relish quiet after what's happened."

"No problem. Are you here about the estate sale?"

Margaret tightened her grip on her black handbag. "I have a proposal for you."

"If you'd like to come on the first day of the sale with the dealers and the shop owners, you're welcome."

"I have a better offer. My friends and I want to form a co-op and sell from Now and Then. Of course, we'll buy the shop."

"Buy the store?" Surprise stole the rest of Ela's words.

"I learned an aggressive developer bought the block before Now and Then and plans a mini mall. The old neighborhood is about to become alive again. Don't worry. We'll give you fair value for your property."

"I'm thrilled to sell. My realtor, Kevin, will handle the paperwork."

"I have one more request. We want to hire you as the manager. We don't know the first thing about running a business."

"I was a financial advisor, and I've a blemish, a large blemish, on my work history."

"Are you turning me down?" Margaret put her hand over her heart.

"No, Mrs. McCain, I'm just clarifying my qualifications and past." She'd just rattle the truth off to her. What else could she do? "I was under suspicion of financial fraud when I lived in Manhattan."

"Dear, we know all about your problems in New York and that you were cleared. Don't hold onto ancient history. We've too much to do in life."

Ela's brain whirled with her revelation. "You knew about my dad when I went to your home for dinner?" She'd worried for nothing at the meal?

"I did. Your aunt was quite frank about her relatives' troubles with anyone who was interested. Her frankness ended the gossip. People felt it was a personal tragedy." Margaret's eyes grew rounder. "I apologize if my questions at dinner made you uncomfortable. I have always believed when you entertain, you try to show interest in your guests and their lives with questions. Was your father's crime supposed to be a secret in Rockypoint?"

A lightness filled Ela. "Ah, no. I've no secrets. None."

"Good, because we voted for you unanimously. And I'm Margaret. Please, don't forget."

Ela couldn't keep the grin off her face. "I'll cancel the estate sale." She held out her hand. "Thank you, Margaret. I hope your church group still has an opening. My sister and I would love to join."

"Your family is always welcome." The older woman broke into a smile as she accepted Ela's handshake followed by a hug. "Oh, I almost forgot." She dug a vase out of the brown bag on the porch step.

"Nash told me your aunt's was broken. Please accept this replacement."

As Ela held the blue and white porcelain urn a lump formed in her throat, and she mumbled her gratitude.

Margaret slung her purse over her shoulder. "We'll set up a time to discuss contracts." She started to turn away and paused. "My son knows nothing about this. You should tell him before the others do. I'm sure he'd love to hear the news from you first."

"But—"

"No buts," Margaret said before she walked down the sidewalk and slid into her vehicle.

Ela shut the door. Why would Nash want to hear from her first? Her cell phone was resting on the coffee table. She picked it up and hesitated. Finally, she hit the numbers and announced the big news to Suz.

* * *

"Harrington is telling everyone you represent him."

Nash directed his gaze at his father sitting on the other side of the desk. "The man knows how to squeeze publicity for himself out of someone else's tragedy. He was threatening to fire me until he saw the headlines about the arrest."

"And he learned about your role in capturing a criminal."

"Harrington intends to use the buzz for himself." Nash frowned over the memory of the annoying man.

"He offered to put our office on retainer," his father said. "I'll draw up the papers with your permission."

"I'll finish the case, but otherwise, I'm done with Harrington. My life is too short to waste on him and his attitude. Sack me if you want. From now on, the people I love come first."

"Why would I dismiss you? You just promised to spend more time with me when I'm not at the office."

"You're always thinking like a lawyer, Dad."

"The movers come tomorrow. By Monday, we'll start fresh in our new offices."

Nash's phone buzzed. He picked up the receiver. "Yes, Joanne."

"Miss Danforth is here. Should I set up an appointment or will you be free soon?"

Ela was on the other side of the door. After Ballard arrested the Judge, Nash had filled her in on his search for Aaron and how he'd figured out what was going on. But he hadn't seen her in three long weeks.

Nash straightened his tie with one hand. "Have her come in. My father and I are finished."

"We'll talk later," Simon said, rising from his chair.

"Sure." Nash stood and focused on the door. Ela walked in and traded pleasantries with his father, who didn't hide his pleasure over her appearance before he exited. She was as stunning as always.

"Nash, thanks for seeing me." A flush crept over her cheeks.

"How are you?" His heart thumped in his chest.

She clutched her hands together at the waist of her black dress. "Healing quickly."

"Great. How's Suz?"

"She's calmed down after all the excitement. She's with Tyler at school. I'm sure they're proclaiming their undying love. I've accepted that he's not a bad guy. His tears for Suz were real, and he did go off to search for her. I'll give him a chance."

"Did Ballard explain the Judge's connection to Dylan? What was his story?"

She nodded. "Dylan worked for the Judge on his farm in Vermont, and the Judge, aware of Dylan's lack of character, tracked him to Rockypoint to offer him a special job, getting rid of somebody who hurt him and his family. Dylan couldn't refuse the money offered. He accepted the deal and started tailing me in his truck and later in the black sedan. He thought I was in my aunt's car on Moose Hill."

"Of course, it was Suz."

"What's happening with the Judge, Nash?"

"The Judge's lawyer has requested a competency hearing for his client."

"I always felt guilty for not revealing Aaron's plan to run off, but the Judge thought his sons were perfect, and I didn't want to disillusion or hurt him with the truth after Aaron died. I was able to use Aaron's escape plan along with an imaginary letter from him to hold the Judge off long enough for you to arrive."

"Good thinking, Miss Danforth. I, too, was caught up with the Judge. He wrote to me at the memorial website I set up about Aaron and defended his son."

"It's like he was everywhere. I'm so happy I don't have to look over my shoulder all the time. Let's hope the trial is fast. On a couple of happier notes, my mother is hinting she'll return soon, and Suz is teaching a ballet class after school at the studio on Main Street. She finally decided to let me in on the news. Apparently, while helping Tyler find an apartment, she found the job, filling in for a maternity leave beginning now."

"Suz is full of surprises. Lanie told me this morning when she asked me to buy her dance shoes for the class."

"Suz didn't tell me Lanie's her student."

"A teen's got to have her secrets."

"And, Suz and Tyler joined the church's teen group. Their marriage is off the table for a while. The boy does show potential."

"I know you're happy about the wedding delay," Nash said. "Lanie's already gotten her uncle to promise to attend her recital in exchange for both of us attending a few of his team's games. We've called a truce for Lanie's sake."

"I'm glad you're well." The dark shadows below her eyes had vanished. She looked even more eye-catching, the longer she stood in front of him.

"Thank you. You've done so much for us. Suz told me you skipped a meeting with an important client to come to our house the night the Judge attacked me, and how she's a hero because she told you about me skipping my book club, which led to you figuring out I was a target."

"I'm learning what's crucial in my life. It took me a while.

I'm a slow learner. Besides, anyone would have—"

She cupped her hand over his mouth for a second. "I've a gift for you." She dug into her purse and brought out a white candy box. She handed it to him. "Open it."

His mouth watered for fudge and her touch. Since she was waiting for him to remove the lid, he popped it off. Inside lay a brass plaque with his name. He blinked in surprise.

"I remembered you were moving into a new office. A lawyer needs the perfect nameplate over his door." She wet her lips and sobered. "I...I'm sorry for the other day when I condemned all lawyers for my father's problems and when I said you—"

He kissed her quickly and then searched her face. Was she as eager as he to pick up where they'd left off? Maybe the gift was just a goodbye token.

"I'm falling in love with you, Nash," she whispered.

His pulse kicked up. "That works, because I'm already in love with you. It happened when I met you in the hospital hallway."

"You're a smooth talker, McCain." Her face reddened. "You didn't even know me then."

"I do now and I'm going to get us right. The people I love come first. Not many have a second opportunity, but I've been given one." He felt her body tense in his arms and he released her. "What is it?"

"I read my father's letter. I've decided to visit him. Would you go with me? I don't expect a miraculous reconciliation, but I'm willing to try to—forgive."

"You're a brave woman."

She shook her head. "When the Judge attacked me, I thought my life was over. I'm alive for a reason and can't afford to waste my days on blame. I've a lot to prove. I let my tragedies blind me to the goodness around me. For a time, I forgot beliefs and relationships would support me and lead me out of pain. But I was never alone. I had Suz, you and your family. And yes, maybe a guardian angel."

"Lanie will approve." He reached for her hand and tucked it between his.

She edged closer to him. "People I never met reached out to me. I realize how blessed I am, and I've a lot to pay forward."

"We've both a lot of living and thanking to do." He intended to appreciate her every day.

"And I'm going into business with your mother and friends at Now and Then."

"My mother? Like I said, you're a brave woman." He tugged her tight against his chest and tipped her chin upward. "I'm crazy about you, Michaela Danforth."

"You'd better be, McCain." A teasing smile lit her face. "So are you ready to take on a household of three women—me, Lanie and Suz? *You're* the brave one, Nash." She stretched up on tiptoes and kissed him.

THE END

A WORD ABOUT THE AUTHOR...

Nora LeDuc is the author of eleven published books. She lives in New England with her family. She's hard at work on her next romantic suspense novel *The Girls of Pretty Park*.

She would love to hear from you.
NoraLeDuc@yahoo.com

And be sure to check Nora's website:
NoraLeDuc.com